THE SPIDER:
BLIGHT OF THE BLAZING EYE

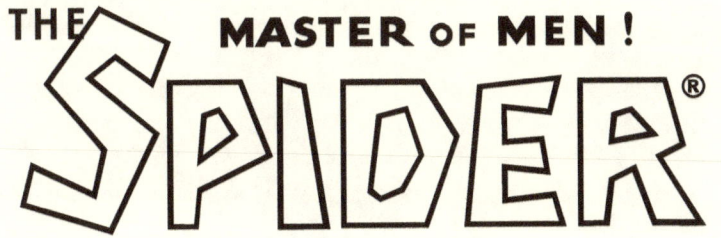

THE **MASTER** OF **MEN !**

SPIDER®

BLIGHT OF
THE BLAZING EYE

By Grant Stockbridge

POPULAR PUBLICATIONS • 2022

CHAPTER 1
TRAILING CURSE

"**F**RED HAD a premonition of death that night; I could read it on his face, in the uneasy depths of his eyes, even though he said nothing about it. I tried to get him to go out with me, wanted to take him to a show—but he insisted that he was tired and would rather turn in early. He was *afraid.* That was why he stayed there in his room—*and his very fear doomed him.*" There was haunting dread in Morton Cramer's demeanor as the low-spoken, half-hesitant words fell from his lips. Within less than a month Cramer had seen death reach out unexpectedly and mysteriously to snatch four of his companions; and the experience had made him jumpy, a man who seemed to be watching furtively for danger that might leap out at him from any corner. Broad-shouldered, square-faced, about thirty, his dark eyes shifted from one to the other of his auditors and then stared off into shadow-haunted space.

"You know the rest," he said softly. "He burned to death in his bed. Set the mattress on fire with a cigarette, they decided at the coroner's inquest—"

"But Fred Powell didn't smoke," Richard Wentworth's resonant voice clipped incisively. "The day before he left with you fellows he came here to thank me for helping him get the job. He laughed about his inability to smoke that day—told me a cigarette always made him as sick as a youngster who had

1

slipped out behind the barn to make his first experiments with nicotine. Certainly he never would have smoked in bed. That was badly out of character—a careless slip on the part of whoever is responsible for these deaths, these murders—"

Wentworth's keen, blue-gray eyes peered thoughtfully from their deep sockets. His flat-planed, vitally handsome face was stern and grim-lipped, as his gaze strayed abstractedly out of the window of his Sutton Place living room and settled unseeingly over the dusk-shrouded surface of the East River flowing silently three floors below. A poker face—but behind it his alert faculties were at work, probing, searching, tearing away all blinding pretense.

In that moment he was inwardly transformed from the immaculately-clad, seemingly indolent clubman that he appeared, into that denizen of the darkness men knew as the Spider. In what purported to be an accidental death, his crime-attuned nostrils had scented murder—and now every instinct of the manhunter was stimulated.

"Murder?" Nita van Sloan repeated the ugly word with a tremor of anxiety, as her violet eyes scrutinized his face. "You mean that Fred was killed—that his body was cremated in order to conceal what had been done?"

That word "murder" had sounded an instinctive alarm in her brain, had stabbed into her heart. For she knew all too well the reaction it would bring forth from Richard Wentworth, the man she loved better than all the world, better than life itself. His blood would pound in his veins at the thought of a friend who had been killed without a chance to defend himself. Righ-

2

Through the holocaust loomed
the incredible figure!

teous indignation would surge through him at the spectacle of triumphant lawlessness.

Many times she had seen that challenge take the Spider deep

into the shadow of death—and now, once more, she could see the battle light kindling in the depths of his eyes....

ABOUT FOUR months previously young Fred Powell, an enthusiastic, adventure-hungry radio operator, had sat there in the spacious living room of Wentworth's Sutton Place home. His boyish face had been wreathed with delight as he envisioned what lay ahead of him.

Through Wentworth's introduction and recommendation, Powell had been engaged to go with the Alden-Harmon Expedition to explore Central Asia by air. Wentworth had two acquaintances in the expedition's personnel—Peter Ellison, a pilot, and Morton Cramer, a radio operator. Through them Wentworth had negotiated Powell's appointment—and unknowingly had sent the laughing-eyed youngster to his death. All had gone well with the expedition in Asia. After two months of flying and highly successful exploration in Mongolia and Tibet, they had flown back to Singapore and prepared to start home by boat. It was then that disaster first struck. While returning to their hotel at night, Peter Ellison, and Andrew Thompson, one of the scientists of the party, had been pounced upon by natives who leaped at them from a dark alley. Ellison had managed to beat off the attackers, but Thompson had been stabbed to death.

Apparently that had been nothing more than the usual robbery-motivated waylaying—but within a week Thompson had been followed in death by Bert Hardy, a fellow scientist. Hardy had not appeared for breakfast on the fourth day out from Singapore. When his friends went to investigate, they found that his berth had not been slept in—nor was there any sign of him when the ship had been searched from stem to stern. Bert Hardy had gone overboard sometime during the night....

Ted Newsome had been the third to die—in an agony of convulsions that the ship's physician pronounced the result of ptomaine poisoning. And Fred Powell had been number four.

Four deaths among the ten white men who had composed the expedition—that had been all the newspapers of the country needed. For the past two weeks they had been headlining stories of the "curse" that had been following the Alden-Harmon Expedition—a curse supposedly invoked because the explorers had violated a native tabu. The picture of a vengeful Asiatic doom, cutting down man after man, made excellent material for sensational newspaper stories. But Wentworth was not interested in fiction.

"Powell knew that those first three deaths were not merely accidental," he said with conviction. "He must have suspected that he was scheduled to die—might even have suspected the nature of the doom that threatened him."

"He must have had a premonition of death," Cramer repeated. "That was why he asked me to bring this prayer wheel to Miss van Sloan—if anything happened to him. But if he had any suspicion of what his danger might be, he said nothing about it."

On the table beside Nita stood a frail creation of teakwood about a foot high; a miniature water wheel with bits of ideograph-inscribed paper attached to its paddles—prayers which fluttered in the air when her fingers gently flicked the spokes and set the wheel in motion. The present Fred Powell had brought back from the Orient for her but had never been able to deliver.

As it creaked softly it seemed to be trying to tell them the secret of his death—but the whirring whisper was abruptly blotted out by the clamor of the telephone.

Wentworth stepped to the instrument, lifted the receiver—and instantly a man's deep voice rumbled at him over the telephone wire.

"This is Ellison—Peter Ellison, Wentworth!" it babbled incoherently. "I'm going to be the next to die—I know it! It's that damned eye! They found it and took it away—but it's back here in my room! It's blazing down at me and burning me up! I'm on fire, Wentworth—*burning up inside!* God Almighty, help me, man—*help me!*"

Wild terror throbbed through that hoarse rumble—inconceivable, coming from the tough, hard-bitten pilot-adventurer.

"Steady, Ellison—pull yourself together!" Wentworth cut into the terrified babble; but the pilot did not seem to hear him.

The frenzied pleading suddenly ended in a scream of excruciating agony.

Cramer, standing at Wentworth's side, heard that scream, and became livid. His forehead was beaded with perspiration as he tried to regain control of his voice.

"He knew that it was coming!" He sank back into his chair. "He knew that he was in constant danger, and it had him terrified. I tried to get him to talk, but he shut up like a clam whenever I questioned him. He was being threatened—and did not dare say so. Now they've got him—"

"You have your car downstairs, haven't you?" Wentworth demanded, as he half-dragged the trembling man to the door.

"We'll use that. There may still be a chance for Ellison—if we can get there at once."

For an instant his glance met Nita van Sloan's—and she understood. He was going into danger. She wanted to be at his side when he faced it—but this was not a time when she could help him. This was one of the times when she must remain behind—to wait and wonder.

"Please stay here, Nita," he asked simply. "I will be back as soon as I can." And then he was gone, and she was alone with the little wheel that turned almost soundlessly, the whirring flutter of its prayers echoing the silent pleas for his safety that went up from her heart....

MORTON CRAMER seemed to have recovered his self-control by the time they reached the street. He led the way on the run to his coupé and flung himself behind the wheel. The car headed downtown toward Peter Ellison's Gramercy Park apartment, but before they had gone a dozen blocks Wentworth saw that the radioman was actually unnerved. Clutching the wheel as if he feared it might wrest itself from his hands, he seemed oblivious to his surroundings.

Past two red lights the car sped before a shrill whistle sounded behind them. A red-faced traffic cop came running up when traffic congestion made them come to a stop. Then, instead of keeping his head, Cramer started to abuse the officer for detaining them.

"This is a matter of life and death—and you hold us here with your fool red tape!" he stormed. "I'll see to it that you catch plenty of hell for this!"

That was a mistake. The officer's red face became crimson, and he started to get into the car, to take them to the precinct station. It took all of Wentworth's diplomacy, and the flashing of a card which identified him as a friend of the police commissioner, to cool the man's anger—and even then they were detained until he had written out a ticket for Cramer.

Instead of making him more cautious, that delay only added to the radioman's nervous recklessness. Within a few blocks the car swerved wildly and almost climbed the sidewalk in order to avoid a collision. Wentworth waited for no more.

"I'll take the wheel before you add yourself to the Alden-Harmon death list," he snapped, as he shouldered Cramer aside and swung the car back into the center of the street.

Meekly Cramer slumped back on the seat, but his eyes peered through the windshield anxiously as they turned into East Twenty-first Street. The sedate neighborhood of the park showed no evidence of excitement, and the building in which Ellison lived was quiet when they arrived.

There was no response to their ring, but Wentworth's skeleton keys made quick work of the outer door. An automatic elevator took them up to the fourth floor—and the moment they stepped out into the hallway Wentworth tensed... tensed and sniffed. The hair at the back of his neck seemed to stand on end and a chill trickled down his spine as his nostrils filled with the unmistakable stench of burned flesh!

Cramer caught that nauseating odor, too. White-faced and trembling, he led the way to Ellison's apartment, then stood back while the skeleton keys probed.

The moment the door opened that choking stench assailed them even more strongly. Wentworth caught a red flicker that came from a room at the end of the long, narrow inner corridor. The flicker of flames!

Quickly he ran down the corridor and into the wildly disordered living room, where dancing flames were beginning to eat their way across the rug. His hand reached for the switch, and when the lights snapped on his eyes turned to the middle of that patch of flames and beheld all that remained of Peter Ellison— *an unrecognizable charred skeleton!*

"God, he's burned to a crisp!" Cramer gasped from behind him. "Just like Fred Powell—burned away to nothing!"

But Wentworth was staring down at that charred horror with wide, puzzled eyes. Ellison's clothing had been burned away; all but a few remnants that still smoldered where they had fallen from the bones. His flesh had been utterly consumed, until what remained was nothing more than a red-smoldering crust on the charred bones—and yet the fire that had cremated his body so completely was just beginning to spread across the rug and ignite the rest of the thoroughly ransacked room!

It was impossible that fire blazing fiercely enough to consume human flesh so completely would not have enveloped the entire room and set the building on fire—and yet, there was the amazing evidence of it!

For a moment the astounding sight held Wentworth spellbound. Then he went to work. Cramer was on the verge of collapse from fright and horror. He was almost useless in helping to check the blaze, but Wentworth managed to beat out the flames before they had made much more headway.

There was nothing more he could do for the grisly corpse on the floor, nothing but notify the police and wait to tell them of Ellison's futile call for help. While he awaited their arrival he made a thorough search of the apartment, but it yielded nothing that was of value in establishing how Ellison had met his death or indicating the identity of his killers.

Wentworth had no doubt that the man had been murdered—but how he had been killed now promised to remain an unsolved mystery, the answer destroyed with his consumed flesh. The apartment had been thoroughly ransacked, had been turned upside down in a search for something evidently of small size—but whether or not the searcher had found what he wanted was another question for which there seemed little hope of an answer.

"—that damned eye—they found it and took it away—but it's back here in my room," Ellison's frenzied words surged back into his mind. "It's blazing down on me and burning me up—"

Mad, unintelligible words that made no sense....

Wentworth was still mulling over them when Inspector Farragut arrived with a detail of detectives. An acquaintance of Wentworth's, the inspector listened to his account and stared down at the charred skeleton with popping eyes.

"That body was burned somewhere else and then brought here," he declared positively. "There's no other way the flesh

10

could have been consumed so thoroughly—not without burning down the whole building. That must have left the trail we can follow."

But when his men investigated they discovered not the slightest evidence of a trail; discovered, instead, half a dozen circumstances which established conclusively that the charred skeleton could not have been brought into the building. The body must have burned away to nothing there in the middle of that room that had only started to burn when there was no more flesh upon which the amazing flames could feed!

WENTWORTH DID not wait for that investigation to be completed. As soon as Farragut was finished questioning them, he and Cramer left the police-thronged apartment. The fear of death seemed to weigh heavily on the radioman, and he gratefully accepted Wentworth's offer to accompany him to his Tudor City apartment hotel rooms, where he had to change clothes for the reception to the Alden-Harmon party which was to be held that evening.

"This thing is beginning to get me," he confessed, as he nervously mopped his brow. "Thompson, Hardy, Newsome, Powell, and now Ellison—it almost looks as if there is something to this curse business!"

Wentworth took no stock in curses, but now that five of the ten members of the Alden-Harmon Expedition had met tragic fates he could not blame Cramer for his fear. After the sight that had met their eyes in Ellison's apartment, there was no telling what might await them in Cramer's quarters. Wentworth was prepared for most anything—but not for the welcome that met them even before they entered the building....

The street was empty when Cramer left his coupé in a parking space and started toward the wide entrance—except for a car that stood at the curb near the corner. The click of their heels echoed hollowly in the still evening air—the only sound until suddenly something whistled past Wentworth's cheek and thudded into the side of the doorway within scant inches of Cramer's head. Thudded into the doorway and quivered there for an instant before it burst into flames.

That something was a knife—an Oriental-handled knife that had streaked at them from out of the darkness!

With split-second speed Wentworth whirled and flung himself into a crouch, but fast as he was, the would-be assassins were faster. There were two of them—two yellow-skinned, slant-eyed men who flung themselves into the opened door of the waiting car before his blazing guns could bring them down. Grimly he pumped lead after them, but the car leaped away from the curb even before its passengers were through the doorway, and in another moment they were safely out of range.

Hard-eyed and tight-lipped, he turned back to where Cramer stood gaping at the weapon that almost had found a sheath in his neck. Now the Chinese-carved handle was blazing fiercely, the red flame tongues even licking up and down the razor-sharp blade. It would wipe clear of any telltale fingerprints, Wentworth understood.

"Never mind the knife—let's get out of here before a crowd collects," he commanded swiftly.

Cramer led the way inside and upstairs. Nervously he glanced at Wentworth as he fumbled for his keys and unlocked the apartment door. Timorously he pushed it back and felt for the light switch. Then he leaped back the moment the bulb snapped on.

"They've been here, too!" he gasped—but Wentworth was already past him, guns ready as he leaped into the disordered apartment.

Everything in the two-room suite was topsy-turvy, but this time there was no sickening odor to greet them and no charred skeleton lay stretched on the floor. The rooms were empty. The intruders evidently had finished their search and departed, leaving no clue to their identity—until Cramer stared down at his disordered desk and picked up a sheet of rice paper that lay in the middle of it.

A thin sheet of rice paper that was stamped with a six-inch square of dead-black ink, out of the center of which a tilted, almond-shaped eye blazed malevolently.

"The eye! That's what Ellison said—the eye!" Cramer chattered, as he clutched the sheet in his trembling fingers and stared at it with bulging eyes. "There it is, Wentworth—*the eye!*"

Wentworth reached for it, but before he could grasp it the paper suddenly burst into flame and was instantly consumed.

"The eye!" Cramer gasped as he stared stupidly at the thin film of ashes on his singed fingers. "I am next, Wentworth—that thing was my death warrant!"

CHAPTER 2
YELLOW DOOM

WHITE-HOT ANGER raged in Richard Wentworth's heart as he turned away from the building that had almost proved to be a death trap for the sixth member of the Alden-Harmon Expedition. Two of his friends had been murdered, and the chill breath of death had blown on the cheek of a third. Cowardly murders that cried out for vengeance!

One of those deaths, he felt, was squarely on his own shoulders. It was he who had sent Fred Powell off to his doom— and it was up to him to see that the cold-blooded killers who had slaughtered him were brought to justice. At first, that had seemed to be an almost hopeless proposition—but now he had a clue; had several clues which all pointed unmistakably in the same direction.

The murderous knife that had just missed Morton Cramer had been of Chinese manufacture. The rice-paper death note was a Chinese product. And the two killers who had made their escape had looked like Chinese. In some way the yellow men were tied up with this doom that pursued his friends. And when there was a Chinese riddle to be solved no man in New York City was better equipped to put his finger on the answer than patriarchal old Moo Fong, the "mayor" of Chinatown.

Wentworth's tall, athletic figure moved quickly as he strode down the street and hailed a cab. A few hours before, he had been carefree and at peace with the world. Crime and sudden death had seemed to be far away from his comfortable living room—until suddenly the charred corpse of Peter Ellison had been literally thrust upon him.

That ghastly discovery and the attack on Morton Cramer that had followed it had stirred his blood and sounded the challenge he could never resist—the challenge of the murderous criminal who brazenly pits himself against society. Whether those killers were white or yellow made no difference; when they made a mockery of law and order it was time for the Spider to come out of his lair.

White or yellow made no difference—but the Spider had matched wits with Oriental master-criminals many times before. He knew the subtle cunning, the colossal scheming and the inhuman cruelty of which the Oriental mind was capable. If a yellow plotter was behind these slayings, there was no telling what the object of the murder campaign might be or where it would end....

But old Moo Fong should know if anything of that sort was on foot. Very little transpired in the narrow alleys and the hidden burrows of Chinatown that did not come to his attention—and never had he refused his aid to the trusted "white brother" who had more than once proved himself an invaluable friend to the yellow men. Moo Fong would know the meaning of that blazing-eye warning and the explanation of the weird fire that consumed human flesh and yet barely ignited inflammable material all around it....

Wentworth left the cab in Chatham Square and went the rest of the way on foot. Almost immediately he was glad that he had taken that precaution. Something was wrong there in the congested Chinese districts; something was not as it should be. He detected that before he had walked a block; felt his nerves tingling in sub-conscious rapport with the suppressed excitement he sensed all around him.

Not that there was anything outwardly wrong. The patrolman paced his beat as usual, a few sightseers walked through the narrow streets gazing up curiously at the dark house-fronts that were little different from those in the rest of the city, a sightseeing bus stopped to unload its passengers and lead them to a tearoom. All that was usual and as it should be—and yet the strange sixth sense that so often had served Wentworth in good stead whispered a warning.

It was the Chinese on the street who were different. Instead of ignoring the whites with their usual indifference, they were scrutinizing each passerby carefully; scrutinizing them covertly but with sharp eyes that missed nothing.

Eyes… Wentworth could feel them boring into his back; could feel them watching his every move. Eyes not only out there on the street, but from the dark windows all around him. Suspicious, hostile eyes that reminded him of the single flaming optic on Morton Cramer's death warning….

They followed him to the front of Moo Fong's four-storied building, and even when he was admitted, and the door closed behind him, he felt that their searching scrutiny still trailed him. But now there was a new sensation that impressed him the moment the door opened and a smiling Chinese bowed low to admit him… A sensation of something wrong; there was something wrong about that fellow—Wentworth knew it at once.

Moo Fong's doorman was not always the same. Wentworth had been admitted by several, but there was one quality that characterized them all—a certain dignity of bearing that did honor to their master at the same time that they welcomed the visitor. It was as if they never allowed themselves to forget that they were Moo Fong's men, servitors favored above all others in the Chinatown colony.

But this fellow was different—fawning, with an artificial smile too unctuous to be deceiving.

"Mr. Richard Wentworth," he repeated in a voice that bore hardly a trace of an accent. "That honorable name is familiar even to my humble ears. Moo Fong will be delighted to hear that you have honored him by this visit. He will be desolated only because it is necessary to ask you to wait until he prepares to greet you. If you will please to follow me?"

THE FRONT of the street floor of Moo Fong's building was occupied by a display room for his importing business. Behind this was his private office, and then a succession of storerooms extending to the rear. To the left of the display room was the doorway which led to the upper floors. It was given over to his private quarters and to the rooms where he transacted the semi-public business of his people.

It was through this doorway that Wentworth had been admitted and up the stairs to the second floor that he followed the silk-garbed servant. Moo Fong's office was simply furnished and as Occidental as he could make it, but the rest of the build-

17

ing was thoroughly Chinese. Richly embroidered silk draperies covered the walls, deep rugs muffled the floors, and the illumination came from electric bulbs covered by little colored lanterns.

The light from those lanterns was fitful and seemed to populate every nook and corner with hovering shadows; a deceptive light that tricked Wentworth's alertly watchful eyes. Twice he thought he saw dark faces peering at him as he followed the servant down a short corridor to a rear room.

That was a face that had disappeared behind that silken curtain at the end of the hall. There were eyes watching his every step; men waiting in hiding to spring the trap into which he was walking. Not a sound betrayed their presence. The house was utterly still—and yet he knew that they were there!

Now the servant had reached the door of the room at the end of the corridor. A small, dimly lighted reception room, Wentworth saw at a glance—and at the same instant he noticed something else. The silken drapery at one side of the room was still moving, still swaying ever so slightly, but only from the floor to a point about three feet above it—a point where a hand on the other side was holding it to still the betraying movement!

There was a man behind that drapery—and there were other men concealed in that room. Wentworth flashed a glance at the smiling face of the servant and knew that his suspicion was correct; the telltale gleam in those dark eyes gave away the ambush.

Too late the fellow realized that he had betrayed himself. Suddenly the masking smile dropped from his face, fear leaped into his eyes. But before he could spring back from the doorway

Wentworth's left hand fastened in the front of his silk blouse and whirled him around. Swept off his feet, the fellow went through that doorway backward, a human shield behind which Wentworth crouched as he charged the barely moving drapery.

Desperately the servant clawed at his belt. His fingers fastened on the hilt of a knife, but before he could use it Wentworth's automatic smashed down on his skull. And then the slumping body sailed across the room, to crash into a brown-skinned Hindu who had materialized out of nowhere—a long knife poised over his shoulder for a deadly throw.

Before the floundering Hindu had hit the floor, Wentworth reached the now-billowing curtain. Savagely he whipped the automatic barrel down at it, again and again—and sprang back out of the way as the body of a squatty Japanese came tumbling into the room.

Chinese, Hindus, Japanese—suddenly that little room seemed to be filled with every breed that Asia ever spawned!

Wentworth's eyes widened in amazement as his gun-barrel thudded down on the skull of a broad-faced Mongol; as he wrested a wicked-looking knife from the hand of a Malaysian and buried it in the fellow's throat. Every breed of Asia—men of races that never had been able to tolerate one another, and yet here they were battling side by side! Age-long enemies united at last, it seemed, in the common urge to slay this white man....

And it was a miracle that they did not succeed in murdering him, in overwhelming him and hacking him to pieces. Wentworth had only one advantage, and that was their number compared to the small size of the room. They got into one anoth-

19

er's way trying to reach him, slashed at one another in their desperate lunges at him.

For his part, Wentworth fought with a cool desperation. His automatic barrels dripped with blood as he flailed at heads and smashed savagely at faces. Batting knives out of brown and yellow hands, he dived to snatch them up and turn them against their former wielders. Catching one of his attackers off guard, he seized the fellow in a *jiu-jitsu* grip and hurled him full at the heads of his mates. Only when the pack threatened to inundate him did he resort to his triggers, and then the room reverberated with thundering death that thrust the Orientals back on their heels.

Carefully Wentworth had been maneuvering toward the door. Now the way was almost clear. Before the attackers could close in again he charged, his head tucked between his shoulders, a human projectile that bowled them off their feet and spilled them in a struggling, squirming heap.

Out into the hallway he dived, raced down the corridor to the stairs—but there half a dozen more Orientals barred his way. A big Hindu was in the lead. From the top of the steps he leaped, a long, wicked-looking knife upraised, sweeping downward.

Wentworth backed away from that charge, his face convulsed with feigned horror. Straight at him the Hindu sprang, and the knife hooked into his coat, slit his sleeve from shoulder to elbow. Blood trickled down his arm and dripped through the slit. But before the brown-skinned man could recover and drive in once more with the knife, Wentworth's fist caught him on the point

of the jaw. That blow lifted him from
his feet and hurled him back down the
stairs upon his fellows.

Now there was no hope of escape by
the stairway, but Wentworth knew Moo Fong's establishment
as few others knew it. Past the stairway he raced and to the front
end of the corridor, where a door opened into the big room the
old man used as an audience chamber.

The door opened when he grasped the knob. Like the smaller
chamber at the rear, this room was dimly lighted, and it seemed
to be empty. Wentworth's heart leaped; that meant that this
way was clear. Quickly he slammed the door behind him and
drew a heavy bolt that fastened it. Then he whirled—and froze
where he stood....

THE ROOM was not deserted, as he had thought. Moo
Fong was there, seated in a big chair on a slightly raised platform
from which he customarily presided over meetings. But at the
first glance Wentworth's eyes widened with horror, and icy cold,
constricting fingers seemed to grip his heart and chill his blood.

Moo Fong was tied in that chair—a ghastly figure with blood
dripping from the empty sockets of his blinded eyes and drool-
ing from his slack-jawed mouth! The old man had been horribly tortured—tortured so barbarously that a shocked gasp burst
from Wentworth's lips.

Not only had the old man's eyes been put out, but his tongue
had been ripped out of his throat! He had been trussed up there
in the seat from which he had once ruled, a butt for the jeers of
his enemies!

21

"Moo Fong, what have those devils done to you, old friend?" Wentworth exclaimed before he realized that the old man could not answer. "This is Wentworth, Moo Fong—"

But even in that extremity Moo Fong was not altogether helpless; even in his insufferable agony his stout heart would not give up. His head lifted and nodded in understanding. The wizened, blood-streaked face twisted into a pathetic gargoyle attempt at a smile—and the yellow, parchment-like eyelids moved up and down over the ghastly empty sockets.

Wentworth stared in horror—and then suddenly he understood. Moo Fong was talking to him; was blinking his lids in the long and short dashes of the Morse code!

"Genghis Khan—destroying—city—everything," Wentworth spelled out the amazing message. *"Tonight—Carnegie Hall—"*

A gleaming knife put a stop to that disclosure. Past Wentworth's face it streaked and plunged deep into the old man's throat, to pin his head back against his chair. The sightless eyes opened wide in a spasm of agony, and when they closed again Wentworth knew that the lids would flutter no more. But before that he had whirled, to blast two bullets through the forehead of the treacherous Chinese servant who had known a way into this room and had used it to creep up and murder his helpless master.

"That makes one of them, Moo Fong," Wentworth's voice was husky and choked as he leaned over the dying man and patted his withered hand. "But there will be more—many more. Until the devils who did this to you have paid in full, I will have no rest!"

And as he turned away from the still corpse he promised

himself that no oath of vengeance he ever had taken would be more faithfully kept. He was sorely tempted to remain there behind Moo Fong's chair and cut down the inhuman devils as they forced a way into the audience room, but against such odds he would have no chance. They would surround him and cut him down—and now he had no right to take unnecessary chances with his life.

"Carnegie Hall—tonight," Moo Fong's dying message coursed through his brain. Carnegie Hall—that was where the reception for the members of the Alden-Harmon Expedition was to be held!

What Genghis Khan could have to do with that reception in Carnegie Hall he had not the remotest idea. Moo Fong's cryptic warning seemed to make no sense whatever....

Wentworth glanced at the tortured corpse of the old Chinaman, and an involuntary shudder coursed through him. Fiends who were capable of such barbaric treatment of a helpless old man—what hellish, unthinkable atrocities might their twisted brains not conceive? What horrifying outrage might they not be preparing to perpetrate on the unsuspecting audience that had gathered to greet the returned explorers?

A glance at his watch told him that it was nearly eight-thirty. By now the Carnegie Hall auditorium would be well-filled, the program ready to begin—and he, the only one who could warn them of the unknown danger that hung over them, was miles away.

That meant that he had not a moment to lose. Moo Fong's avenging would have to wait. Now his only hope lay in flight—

immediate flight before these bloodthirsty Orientals could break in and trap him.

SWIFTLY HE ran behind the platform and pushed a way through the silk draperies at its rear. Beyond them his pencil-flashlight revealed a little alcove that was empty except for an overturned chair and the sprawled body of a Chinese servitor. The man's throat had been slashed from ear to ear, his head almost severed from his shoulders. Moo Fong's bodyguard had been true to his trust; had died there in the observation post outside the audience room.

Wentworth lifted the body to one side and pressed his fingers against two panels in the wall. Noiselessly a section

In a flash the auditorium became a blazing inferno as the conflagration leaped from on human bonfire to another!

of the hardwood floor began to lower at one end as if it worked on well-oiled hinges, a section two feet wide and eight feet long. When it came to rest on the floor below, certain of the hardwood strips in the parquet design shoved partway out from the rest—and formed the ladder which Moo Fong had provided to give him an emergency exit

That ladder led down into a clothes closet at one side of the old man's private office. There Wentworth again pressed a panel, and the ladder silently rose and moved back into its place.

Now he was free—but just as he was about to open the closet door he stopped his hand. His keen ears had caught sounds out there in the office—the sound of running feet coming from the direction of the storerooms. So someone else knew of this secret exit and was leading the Orientals downstairs to head him off!

But wise old Moo Fong had provided even for this contingency. Again Wentworth's pencil-flash speared the stygian darkness of the closet's interior and located a hook on the wall beside him. Grasping it firmly, he pulled it downward and thrilled with satisfaction as the floor beneath him began to move.

More than that, the lever he had operated had released a small panel that glided back to reveal a compact arsenal behind the closet wall. Automatics, knives—and half a dozen high-powered hand grenades!

Fists were pounding on the closet door, tugging at it and trying to force it open, but the noise quickly faded—for Wentworth was no longer in the cubbyhole. A section of the back wall and the floor had turned completely around, and now he was out in the hallway, just beyond the stairs that led to the second floor.

Clutching two of those deadly grenades in his hands, he stepped out into the corridor and cat-footed toward the door. The hallway was empty, but before he reached the foot of the stairs a swarm of Orientals came charging down, intent on blocking every exit to prevent his escape. In the lead was a tall Eurasian who shouted in amazement as he caught sight of the fugitive—but the warning shout died on his lips.

Grimly Wentworth drew back his arm and sent one of the grenades sailing straight at the stairway. The explosion was thunderous; the concussion so terrific that it knocked him to his knees. But when he staggered back to his feet the entire stairway and all the wall beside it had disappeared. Where those murder-lusting Orientals had been was nothing but a dust-shrouded heap of tumbling debris that echoed with groans of agony.

One more his arm went back—and the second grenade arced through the shattered wall into Moo Fong's office, to complete the work of destruction and demoralization.

"That makes nearly a dozen more, Moo Fong," he muttered, as he tugged open the outer door and darted out into the hushed street. "A dozen more—but your account will not be settled until I know that the kingpin has gone down with the rest."

Those roaring explosions had brought the street to a standstill. Every eye was turned toward Moo Fong's building, and half a dozen Chinese started toward it when the door opened and Wentworth darted out. They started toward it, but that was all. One glimpse of his tense face, of the ready automatic he clutched, was sufficient to send them scurrying back into the shadows from which they had suddenly materialized. In another moment he was in the midst of a group of gaping-mouthed sightseers; was running with them when panic seized them and they took to their heels.

Those grenades had been doubly useful, he exulted, as a taxi-cab sped him uptown to Carnegie Hall. Not only had they helped to avenge old Moo Fong's murder, but the explosions would bring the police swarming into the building; would give the survivors of that wolf-pack plenty to do to explain his mangled corpse.

Moo Fong's dead hand had reached back from the grave to settle with the men who had tortured and killed him. Now would it still point the way to the master-murderer who had ordered his death? Perhaps that was why the dying old fighter had rallied his strength to blink out that final warning. Perhaps the inhuman fiend was to be there in Carnegie Hall?

WENTWORTH EYED the hands of his watch as they fairly raced around the dial. Everything possible seemed to delay that cab, even though the driver was doing his best to earn the bonus he had been promised for speed. Twenty minutes to nine—ten to nine—nine o'clock… and still the Fifty-seventh Street auditorium was blocks away.

Five after nine, ten after… At last the cabbie pulled up at the door and Wentworth leaped out, to breathe a sigh of relief when he saw that there was no sign of trouble around the building. A few late arrivals were still in the lobby around the ticket window. Wentworth joined them and then stepped into the auditorium to wait at the rear for an usher to direct him to his seat

The program was already under way. Seated on the stage were the members of the reception committee and the five survivors of the Alden-Harmon party. Ansel Alden, the expedition's leader, was in the midst of his address, the audience listening attentively.

Wentworth studied them closely: a high-class audience that nearly filled the auditorium. Among them he picked out several turbaned Hindus, spied several Chinese and at least one Japanese. Men of culture, all of them—but some of the world's most dangerous criminals had been men of culture.

From the shadows at the rear of the auditorium he tried to study the faces of those Orientals, tried to detect some telltale indication of suppressed excitement; but there was none. Everything seemed so decorous and peaceful that it was rather ridiculous to be standing there waiting for inexplicable doom to burst over the hall. He heard a click just behind him.

Wentworth whirled. That click—it was the floor-bolt which locked the door through which he had just come. But why should the doors be locked? There were still plenty of seats; no reason for barring latecomers—and no reason for locking the audience inside. Unless it was to prevent them from escaping!

Instantly he sprang to the door and peered through the little square of glass—just in time to catch a glimpse of a dark-skinned face as the man who had fastened the door darted out of view. The broad-featured face of a Mongolian or a Tibetan!

Wentworth waited for no more. Whirling from the door, he ran down into the center of the aisle.

"Watch yourselves!" he shouted. "You are in danger! The doors of this auditorium have been locked—"

Before he could finish, the lights went out and the auditorium was plunged into total darkness… only for an instant. Then a great, almond-shaped eye blazed out on the wall at the back of the proscenium arch, a livid eye that seemed to glare at them balefully.

Instantly the hall became a babel of screams and shouts; terrified screams of women that turned to shrieks of agony as they leaped to their feet and tried to battle a way toward the aisles.

"Down! Down on the floor!" Wentworth shouted, as he flung himself to his hands and knees. "Don't lose your heads or you are doomed! Get down on your knees behind your seats and creep into the aisles—that's your only chance! Some of you men—this way and give me a hand!"

His booming voice carried above the awful din, and its reassuring ring partially allayed the wild panic. In the darkness he felt moving forms, men creeping toward the sound of his voice.

"All right—follow me up to the door. We will have to smash our way out," he directed calmly, and led the way up the aisle.

Now the raging din all around him had become appalling. The shrieks of men were added to the piercing cries of the women. Bodies hurtled over the creeping forms, tumbled into the aisles, tried to stampede madly toward the doors.

"Push them back out of the way," Wentworth commanded. "Knock them down—anything so long as you keep them from piling up at the door and blocking our way. That will mean death for all of us."

"Fire! Fire!" a man's frenzied voice added to the fearful panic. "I'm on fire! I'm burning up inside! For God's sake—let me out!"

Like a mad bull he came charging up the aisle, until Wentworth's arms closed around his legs and pulled him down. Now the double doors were only a half dozen feet away. Wentworth halted his men, lined three of them up beside him and the others behind them.

"All together—now!" he called—and they leaped forward and threw themselves headlong.

The bolts snapped under that impact and the doors flew wide, spilling the charging men out into the darkened lobby. Instantly Wentworth was on his feet, leading the way to the outer doors, throwing them open to admit light from the street. Then he was back at another of the inner doors, drawing the bolts and throwing the doors open. With his pocket-flash waving over his head as a beacon, he shouted above the din—and then went down under the wild stampede that swept up the aisle.

Knocked down and trampled underfoot, Wentworth was almost killed in that frenzied charge. But he managed to crawl to one side and get to his feet; managed to get to the outer door and help hundreds of others to extricate themselves from the press. By then, the street was filled with hysterical survivors. Policemen were battling at his side to save those who were knocked down. The clang of ambulances was added to the keening sirens of arriving patrol cars.

Once more Wentworth fought his way back to the doors

of the auditorium—but this time there was little he could do for those who were trapped inside. Fire had broken out among them.

In a flash the auditorium became a blazing inferno as the conflagration leaped from one human bonfire to another! A blazing inferno in which hundreds of trapped victims were being consumed!

Waves of blistering flame drove Wentworth back from that doorway, and as he retreated he took with him the unforgettable picture of that malevolent eye blazing down on the horror beneath it. The blazing eye—the same that had stared up from the death notice Morton Cramer received; the same that Peter Ellison had shrieked about before he burned to death....

Moo Fong must have known about that eye. It was due to his timely warning that Wentworth had been able to save more than half of that trapped audience from a frightful death. He had at least partially circumvented this fiendish deviltry. But as he turned away from the blazing building where he could be of no more use his brain seethed with bitter rage.

In the morning the newspapers would be filled with stories of the malevolent curse that dogged the footsteps of the Alden-Harmon party. But this ghastly outrage was entirely the work of human hands; of cold-blooded human fiends who were using that supposed curse as a smokescreen for something so terrible that its enormity stunned him. Something so potent that it was able to unite the age-old enemy elements of the yellow race into a brotherhood of wanton murder and turn them loose on New York....

CHAPTER 3
NEXT TO DIE

TRUE TO Wentworth's expectation, the newspapers unanimously headlined fantastic stories of the Asiatic curse the next morning in recounting the ghastly tragedy at Carnegie Hall, but the fallacy of that wild theory came home to him as he sat in the office of Police Commissioner Stanley Kirkpatrick and regarded the others who had been summoned there for a conference with the police. Those others were the surviving members of the Alden-Harmon Expedition, the men on whom the blight of this weird curse was supposed to have fallen.

Not one of them had lost his life in the Carnegie tragedy. Safe on the stage, they had not been swallowed up in the frenzied stampede but had made their escape from the hall by a rear exit. It was the innocent audience who had done nothing to invoke the curse who had been its victims.

If the fiend who had decreed that horrible slaughter was there in the auditorium when it took place, the safest place for him would have been on the platform, Wentworth mused. Which meant that he must be one of the eminently respectable members of the reception committee—or one of these men who were gathered there now in the commissioner's office....

One by one, Wentworth regarded them, studied them searchingly.

First of all, Ansel Alden, a big man of about forty, with flinty eyes that looked out from beneath shaggy brows. A prominent nose and a heavy, blunt chin abetted the eyes in giving him the look of a tenacious bulldog, a man who would tackle anything in his line—and would see it through to the end. Alden, who had been the active head of the expedition, was a widely known and thoroughly experienced explorer to whom the remote places of the earth were no more strange than are the outlying districts of his town to a city-dweller.

Alden sat back in his chair and gazed around the room impatiently, his manner bored and slightly contemptuous.

Across from him sat Morton Cramer, the radio operator. He, too, had a reputation for courage and daring that had been tested more than once by hardship and the threat of almost certain death. Each time Cramer had come through with distinction—but now he seemed shaken. He had recovered somewhat from his uneasiness of the night before, but Wentworth could detect the tense excitement he fought hard to keep under control.

Next to Cramer was Raymond Millar, an aviator who was a graduate of the transcontinental service. A man of about thirty-five, with a broad, phlegmatic face, Millar looked like the type of whom nothing could disturb—but in him, also Wentworth detected uneasiness. His glance darted nervously about the office, like that of a wild thing newly placed in captivity.

James Kennedy, a navigator, was the handsomest man of the outfit. Tall and dark, with wavy black hair, he was the motion picture ideal of what a flyer should be. Leisurely smoking a cigarette, he seemed to be completely at his ease as he sat talking with Trueman Harmon, the banker who had backed the expedition but had taken no active part in it.

Harmon, one of the city's leading financiers, was a man of

about sixty, gray-haired and partially bald, but otherwise well preserved. His manner was self-confident and assured, his large and somewhat heavy-featured face a bit arrogant and truculent. From time to time he glanced at his heavy-chained watch and then at Kirkpatrick, as if to remind the commissioner that his time was valuable.

Dillon Harmon, his son, completed the gathering. Dillon was a younger and milder edition of his father. The arrogance of the elder Harmon had faded in his countenance to the dreamy placidity of the scholar. A man in his late thirties, he had made considerable reputation as a scientist. It was his interest in Mongolian research that had won his father's backing for the expedition, although he, too, had taken no active part in it.

These completed the surviving members of the expedition—with the exception of Christopher Randall, a young scientist, who had not yet arrived for the conference.

The most distinguished-looking man in the room was the police commissioner himself. Handsome, florid, in his late forties, Stanley Kirkpatrick had an air of dignity and authority that was his heritage from years of command. Always immaculately dressed and with his spiked mustache perfectly trimmed, yet there was nothing of the dandy about him—nothing to belie the sterling qualities that were patent in his slightly saturnine countenance.

He was reluctant to begin the conference without Randall, but at last Trueman Harmon's significant watch-snapping seemed to decide him. He reached for his telephone and summoned a detective; ordered him to go to Randall's Greenwich Village rooming house and fetch him.

"Meanwhile, Mr. Alden"—he turned to the explorer—"we may as well begin with you. First of all, I want to know just what happened on this expedition. I want to know everything of significance, everything that might in any way be responsible for these deaths among your party—or for this 'curse' the newspapers are making so much of."

ANSEL ALDEN wasted no words. Briefly and succinctly he outlined the progress of the Alden-Harmon Expedition from the moment when Dillon Harmon had broached the subject, engaged him to head the party and helped to lay out the route to be traversed. The enlisting of the other members, the trip to Asia, the start by air from Shanghai, the progress over Mongolia and Tibet and the wind-up at Singapore—all of these he covered in full detail.

Then a scornful smile flitted over his curled lips.

"I admit that our planes landed in several so-called 'forbidden cities,' among them Lhassa," he finished. "Naturally, we penetrated where no other exploration parties have ever been—but please don't expect me to spin you fairy tales about native curses. The curse bugaboo is nothing but an alibi for men who fall down on their jobs."

"You are certain, then, that you did not incur the enmity of any native or religious group that may have followed your party to this country?" Kirkpatrick persisted. "Both of your planes were together throughout the journey, I assume, Mr. Alden?"

For an instant Ansel Alden hesitated. "We were together at all times—except for one day near Sachi-buluk, in Western Mongolia," he answered. "Ellison left that day for a side-trip to Kur-ogan. Thompson, Newsome, Kennedy and Cramer were with him. They discovered nothing of importance."

His words were dry, matter-of-fact—and yet Wentworth was almost certain that he caught a sardonic gleam in the cold, flinty eyes as the explorer finished and turned to Cramer and Kennedy for confirmation.

Kirkpatrick went on with his questioning, taking one man after the other—but very quickly Wentworth realized that he was getting nowhere. They seemed to answer as best they could, but none of them had a worthwhile suggestion to offer to explain the tragedy in Carnegie Hall or the death of their mates. More and more, as he listened, he became convinced that the active members of the expedition were not telling all they knew; were holding something back—from one another as well as from Kirkpatrick.

Did they know the answer to this death-puzzle? Did they know the significance of the Blazing Eye? Was that why they had all escaped when it turned Carnegie Hall into a ghastly shambles?

Wentworth was striving to read the answers to those questions in their faces, when Kirkpatrick's telephone interrupted his questioning. Over the wire came a heavy, rasping voice that was as clear in the silent office as if each of them had been holding the receiver to his own ear; the voice of Jacobs, the detective Kirkpatrick had sent after Randall.

"We've got another corpse on our hands, Commissioner—or maybe I ought to say what is left of a corpse," he announced. "I just broke into this fellow Randall's room—and I can hardly believe what I saw. There is nothing left of him but a charred skeleton that is spread-eagled on the spring of his bed and held there with handcuffs. It's the damnedest thing! The floor under that bed isn't even scorched, not a fire-mark on it—but his body is burned to a crisp!"

Wentworth watched their faces intently as that news hit them. Watched Alden, and saw the flinty eyes narrow ever so slightly; watched Cramer, and saw the film of perspiration that came out on his taut face; watched Millar, and saw his lips tremble, his tongue come out to wet them nervously; watched Kennedy, and saw his jaws tighten, his lips straighten into a taut line. Now they were four—four out of the original ten; and as Trueman Harmon stared at them the question he asked himself was plain in his eyes: *Which would be the next to die?*

Only Dillon Harmon seemed unimpressed by what he heard. He sat there with a vacant look on his face, as if this swift-moving tragedy was something he could not understand, something not of his world….

THE MOMENT Jacobs hung up, Kirkpatrick flashed the operator and ordered police cars to speed them all to the weird deathbed. Detectives had already combed the one-room-and-kitchenette apartment when they arrived; had searched every inch of it and discovered nothing whatever. There on the blackened bedspring lay the charred skeleton that was all that remained of Chris Randall. From the blackened condition of the handcuffs the police knew that the manacles must have been on his wrists and ankles when his body was consumed. He had been stretched out there on the spring while his flesh burned to a crust on his bones.

"Somebody came in here and stripped the mattress off that bed and stretched him out on it and then—and then set him on fire," Jacobs reconstructed; but Kirkpatrick shook his head in bewilderment.

"It looks as if he has been through the furnace of a crematory," he marveled—and yet he knew that there was nothing in that securely locked apartment that could have been used to roast the flesh from the blackened bones that stared up at him mockingly.

With horror-filled, incredulous eyes the huddled spectators gazed at that uncanny deathbed, and the tongue-tying awe that man feels in the presence of what he considers the supernatural held them speechless. Wide-eyed, they stared—until words that were hardly intelligible started to come from Raymond Millar's blood-drained lips.

"I knew this would happen—I knew it," he mumbled. "Chris knew it, too. He warned me it will get us all—one after the other. We can't escape from it, unless—"

Suddenly he seemed to realize that every eye was turned to him, and the words faded and died on his lips. When Commissioner Kirkpatrick tried to question him further, he shrugged his shoulders helplessly and explained that his nerves were cracking under the strain, that he did not know what he had been saying. But Wentworth's keen eyes had missed no part of that outburst—and he knew that it was a quick, commanding glance from Morton Cramer that had brought Millar up short and silenced him....

Nothing more was to be learned in that gruesome death-room, nothing more to be wrung from the Alden-Harmon survivors, so Kirkpatrick dismissed them. But, at a signal from the commissioner, Wentworth stayed behind after the others had left.

"I can't believe the evidence of my own eyes, Dick," Kirkpatrick worried, when he was alone with the friend with whom he had so often faced the most baffling of criminal problems. "A human body can't burn away to nothing like that by itself—and yet that one *did!* Not only that one, but Peter Ellison's and a hundred and ninety-four others that were trapped last night in Carnegie Hall."

"Was there no chance for an inquest on any of those victims?" Wentworth looked up in quick surprise. "Surely some of those rushed to the hospital were not so badly burned?"

"Despite everything the doctors could do for them, they burned to a crisp—every one of them." The commissioner's voice was low and awestricken, the voice of a man discussing something too shocking for words. "From what was left of

40

RICHARD WENTWORTH ·

Ellison, the doctors could tell nothing—but with the Carnegie victims they were just as helpless. Those bodies burned to a crisp so that not even an autopsy was possible. The best men in the city were summoned, but they are at a loss to explain how the bodies caught fire and were consumed."

"Perhaps a gas or an oil that is highly inflammable," Wentworth now suggested thoughtfully, but Kirkpatrick dismissed that promptly.

"That would burn the skin, would eat in from the outside a ways, but this fire seems to come from within—incredible as that sounds," he explained, as he worriedly brushed his mustache with the first knuckle of his right hand. "We are up against something hellish, Dick—something so incredibly evil that I persuaded the newspapers to hold back the full story of last night's tragedy for fear of creating a panic."

Kirkpatrick was badly worried; Wentworth read that in every line of his tense, haggard-eyed face—but he was worried about something more than he was admitting. Something, Wentworth shrewdly surmised, which he did not dare to mention for fear the admission would bring the Spider to his rescue....

FOR HOURS after he had left Kirkpatrick, that thought rankled in Wentworth's mind. Well he knew the commissioner's antagonism to any interference with what he considered police prerogatives. He appreciated Kirkpatrick's unyielding opposition to the unorthodox methods by which the Spider accomplished his ends and served out relentless justice where the regularly-constituted authorities had failed. Kirkpatrick stood firmly for law and order, with no infringement on the police power no matter how worthy the end or how excellent the results achieved.

For his part, Wentworth acknowledged that the role of the Spider was one to be used only in the greatest emergencies; only when he was convinced that the police were helpless. He would much rather refrain from treading on Kirkpatrick's toes—even when, as now, the memory of his murdered friends cried out to him for justice and revenge.

Already he had done all that he could in this case, he tried to convince himself as he paced his living room and stared down abstractedly at the slow-moving river traffic. This time he would not go out looking for trouble. This time he would leave it to Kirkpatrick—

But even as he reached that decision Jenkyns, his butler, came in to announce that a Miss Viola Dunn would like to see him.

Viola Dunn.... The name was familiar—and so was the slim, dark-eyed, provocative-faced young woman who advanced to meet him with extended hand. Viola Dunn was more than attractive. Under most circumstances she would have been beautiful, but now her eyes were red and sultry. Her face was hard and grim—so bitter that the half-smile she attempted made her look as if she was going to burst into tears.

"You probably do not remember me, Mr. Wentworth," she greeted in a low, husky voice. "I am—I was Peter Ellison's fiancée. That is why I am here—I want your help. Peter can't help himself any longer, and the police are so utterly helpless. A 'curse' killed him!" Her voice vibrated with scorn. "I am surprised that they do not label him a suicide!"

Wentworth led her to a chair and tried to calm her. But her dark eyes were flashing, and hot, impetuous words leaped to her lips.

"Peter Ellison was murdered, Mr. Wentworth—you know that as well as I do," she said levelly, as she leaned forward and looked him straight in the eyes.

"He was murdered in order to get him out of the way, because he knew too much—to close his mouth. He was murdered—and I want to bring his murderer to justice. I want you to help me."

"But if you are so certain that Peter was murdered, there must be someone whom you suspect," Wentworth suggested.

"There is," the girl said bluntly. "Ansel Alden. Something happened on that expedition, Mr. Wentworth. I don't know what it was—Peter only hinted at it to me. But I do know that he was afraid of Ansel Alden. He did not trust the man, and I believe he intended to go to the police with his suspicions—but he never got that chance. I can't prove my suspicions against Alden, but you can; I know your reputation for things of that sort. I want you to do that for Peter—and I want to help you in any way that I can. I want you to promise to call me if there is anything I can do."

In order to calm her, Wentworth promised to investigate Ansel Alden and to call upon her if he discovered any way in which she could be of assistance to him. But when she left he stared thoughtfully at the door that closed after her. He had placed her almost immediately—not as Peter Ellison's fiancée, but as Morton Cramer's. He remembered now that she and Cramer had quarreled and parted, and the engagement to Ellison must have developed subsequently.

If her suspicion of Ansel Alden was correct, Cramer, Millar and Kennedy probably were in deadly peril. If Alden had found it necessary to eliminate six members of his party, they too no doubt were scheduled to die. Cramer was already taking every precaution to protect himself, Millar was thoroughly frightened and would be on his guard, but Kennedy seemed little impressed with the doom that had befallen the others....

Viola Dunn had not gone more than ten minutes when the

44

telephone interrupted Wentworth's meditation. Over the wire came the voice of one of the men of whom he had been thinking.

"This is Raymond Millar, Mr. Wentworth," the speaker announced. "I don't like to intrude on you this way—but I am worried. This morning I wanted to get a word with you, but there was no opportunity. Since then my fears have increased—and now I am sure of them. Twice I caught sight of men shadowing me on the street—once a Hindu and once a Japanese; and just now, as I started to leave my apartment, I spied two Chinese watching the doorway from across the street. Perhaps I am unduly nervous, but after what happened to Randall—"

Into Wentworth's mind flashed a memory of that similar telephone call from Peter Ellison!

"Stay where you are until I get there, Millar," he decided quickly. "I'll be there as fast as a cab can bring me."

THAT TOOK less than fifteen minutes. Wentworth dismissed the cab on the corner and walked the rest of the way to the apartment building, his eyes covertly studying both sides of the street. Yes, Millar had been right; across the way a well-groomed Chinese paced up and down and glanced at his watch impatiently, as if he waited there for an overdue appointment.

Wentworth was relieved; at least this time he had arrived in time and would not walk in on the horror that had greeted him in Ellison's apartment The lobby of the building was empty, and so was the upper hallway when the janitor-elevator operator let him out at the fifth floor and nodded in the direction of Millar's apartment.

At the door Wentworth was about to press the buzzer—when suddenly he stopped and listened. His quick ears had caught the sound of an overturning chair, of a falling body, a groan—and now he heard a warning hiss as someone shushed for silence. Millar was in there—but no longer alone!

Wentworth thought quickly. Moments were precious if Millar was in the danger he feared—yet to open that door might be to walk into a trap. He had to get in some other way... The roof. There were only six stories to this building, he had noticed. Now....

Quickly he located the stairway and sprinted up the remaining flight. Yes, there was a fire escape—one that let down into a courtyard that was darkened by the blank wall of a tall office building next door. Excellent! Carefully he picked his way down the ladder, until he could see into Millar's apartment without being observed from within—and what he saw there clenched his fists and squared his jaw.

The apartment was in the hands of a gang of thugs. Six of them, he counted, and there might be others on guard at the door. They had Millar propped up in a chair, where two of them held him securely. White-faced and with a trickle of blood running down from his split lips, he faced them defiantly; gritted his teeth when a burly thug who seemed to be the leader hauled off and punched him brutally in the face.

"All right, brother," the thug snarled; "I got plenty more where that come from—and you'll keep on getting 'em until you get wise to yourself and spill what we want to know. *Where is it?*"

Wentworth's blood boiled and he took a step toward the window as he saw Millar reel back under that brutal blow—but those thugs were prepared for trouble. Their guns were drawn, ready. Carefully he edged back to the wall of the building and quickly spread a pocket make-up kit on the fire-escape step in front of him. Kneeling in front of it, his fingers went to work swiftly on his face.

Miraculously it was transformed. His cheeks became sallow and deeply lined, his eyes deep-set and glittering, his nose hawklike, his mouth a lipless gash that framed snaggly, discolored teeth. In place of his smooth brows, shaggy, unkempt ones bloomed, and over his head went a wig of straggly, matted black hair. From beneath his vest came a long black cape that tied around his shoulders, a wide, floppy-brimmed black felt hat—and into his hands leaped his twin automatics.

The Spider was ready!

Up to the window he stepped, crouching, ready to smash the pane and leap in with guns naming. But even as his body started forward he checked it and drew back onto his haunches. The door of Millar's apartment had opened and through it poured a swarm of Chinese, Hindus, Mongolians—the living room suddenly seemed filled with them!

So swift was their charge that the thugs were taken unawares; were swept off their feet as gleaming knives slashed at their throats and stabbed at their breasts. But only for an instant. Then their automatics went into action, and flying lead was matched against cold steel.

Millar had the presence of mind to throw his chair over backward so that he could flatten himself on the floor and crawl to one side of that furious battleground. He was between the devil and the deep sea, torture and death his portion no matter which side won. With terrified eyes he watched that deadly struggle—and then fairly leaped out of his skin as another gladiator entered the bloodied arena.

Suddenly the windowpane crashed in, and through it leaped a stooped, twisted, nightmarish creature whose cackling laugh rang out over the thunder of the guns like the weird chuckle of a maniac. An eerie laugh that struck cold terror into the hearts of those murderous battlers—terror that turned to utter panic as his flaming automatics bathed them with lead that decimated their ranks.

Like the swiftly darting insect from which he had taken his name, the Spider scuttled across that room with lightning speed. Ducking, twisting, weaving, he seemed to be in all four corners at once—and from all four corners his automatics chanted their song of death.

"The Spider!" One of the startled thugs howled panic-stricken recognition; and the effect of that dread name was instantaneous.

The Orientals seemed to vanish into thin air, and hot on their heels stampeded the New York gangsters. Into the private corridor and out to the hall the Spider's lead followed them, until they had reached the protection of the stairway and were

in wild flight toward the street. Not until then did he turn back
to the apartment, where Raymond Millar had just gotten trem-
blingly to his feet.

THE FLYER'S eyes were round as saucers as he saw that
incredibly ugly creature scuttling back toward him. His lips
moved soundlessly—and suddenly a scream burst from them
as he clutched at his breast and pitched to the floor, to twitch
and roll over onto his face as a second bullet bored through his
skull! Murderous bullets that had come from the fire escape!

Wentworth had caught the first muffled pop of a silenced
automatic; had glimpsed a handkerchief-masked face that he
was almost certain was Morton Cramer's—and then a third
bullet whistled by his head, a warning of what awaited him if
he tried to pursue through that window.

Such an attempt would be foolhardy, and besides he now had
not a moment to lose in making his getaway. With lightning
speed he got out of the Spider's black habiliments and stripped
off his ugly make-up—but before he could leave that apartment
there still remained a duty he must perform.

Out of his pocket came a little silver cigarette lighter. Swiftly
he bent over the corpses of the three Orientals and the four
white thugs that littered the blood-spattered room—and each
time, in the middle of the dead forehead where he pressed the
bottom of the lighter, a crimson replica of a spider appeared. To
their masters, yellow and white, the Spider served notice that
he intended to put a stop to this ghastly game of murder and
terrorism. This warning would rouse dread!

Who the master of those Orientals might be he had no idea,

but his face hardened as he bent over the dead gangsters. Two of them he recognized—Tuffy Abrams and Joe Ganzi, notorious killers who were well known as henchmen of Nick Penozzi, the white gang-leader who lorded it in the Chatham Square-Chinatown district.

So Nick Penozzi was interested in the Blazing Eye—so interested that he had sent his hoods to extort something from Raymond Millar before the Orientals could reach him! What that something was Millar would now never be able to divulge—but Nick Penozzi knew the answer to that question. Perhaps he also knew the answers to half a dozen other questions that were plaguing Wentworth—answers which he would be most likely to divulge if he were called upon unexpectedly and quickly....

That visit, Wentworth decided, would be the next thing on his program—but when he reached the hallway the elevator indicator told him that the car was just approaching the fifth floor. Downstairs he caught the wail of sirens, the shrill sound of whistles. The police!

Barely in time he reached the stairway door—but up through the stairwell came the sound of pounding feet and gruff voices. That avenue of escape was cut off, and he did not need to be told that they would be swarming up the fire escape. That meant the roof—it was his only refuge. The roof and the water tank!

Fortunately the tank was almost empty. Climbing down into it, he could keep himself above the waterline; could cling there until he heard the police search the roof and go back downstairs. That gave him an opportunity to open the trap and ease his elbows out over the tank cover; but it was hours later, long after dark, before he dared to venture out onto the roof and then down the stairs to hurry through the street.

BY NOW, he feared, Nick Penozzi would he prepared and on his guard, but there might still be a chance of reaching him. A chance worth trying, he decided as he hailed a cab and ordered the driver to take him to Chatham Square. But before he reached his destination the cabman ran into a traffic jam. Ambulances clanged past as they waited to move—and then fire apparatus added to the din.

A fire in Chinatown!

That was all Wentworth needed to know. Dismissing the cab, he mingled with the excited throngs that crowded the narrow streets; worked his way through them until he reached the center of the excitement. The fire was in the Doyer Street Mission, a haven where hundreds of human derelicts were bedded down on the basement floor each night. The building was in flames, but the horrified crowd hardly noticed the blaze.

Dozens of men who tore their clothing from their bodies and screamed that they were being burned alive!

"It musta started down in the basement," an awestricken vagrant muttered to Wentworth. "Most of 'em didn't get out—they burned up down there; but those fellers looks like they're just as bad off."

Wentworth felt his own skin crawl as he watched that fearful agony that nothing could assuage. Most of the victims were beyond speech. They could only moan and squirm horribly—but at that moment two firemen emerged with a big fellow who seemed to be half-mad.

"The eye did it!" he screamed wildly. "The lights went out and then that eye blazed down at us. It burned right into our innards and set us on fire! It's burning me now—worse and worse! I can't stand it!"

Sweat poured down his face in rivulets as he fought frenziedly to break loose before an interne shot a hypodermic injection into his arm and partially quieted him. Sick with horror, Wentworth turned away.

Sudden death by a swift bullet or the sharp blade of a knife was something that could be faced without flinching, but a horrible, agonized end such as had come to those poor vagrants—that was enough to fill the hardest eyes with cringing, enervating terror....

CHAPTER 4
FALSE EYES

NEW YORK journalism had reached a new low, Richard Wentworth disgustedly assured himself the next morning, as he read the accounts of the Doyer Street catastrophe. More than a hundred vagrants had met death in the mission house blaze and yet the papers were filled with stories of a mysterious Asiatic curse that was blamed for the disaster! "The Blight of the Blazing Eye," they dubbed it—and then proceeded to regale their readers with a fantastic story of Oriental cunning and bloodthirstiness.

The Alden-Harmon explorers, according to those accounts, had not only landed in forbidden territory but had violated a

Tibetan temple and had stolen the jewel eyes from a sacred image. As a result, the priests and their satellites had dogged the trail of the expedition. They had followed the explorers all the way back to New York, whittling down the party as they went, fanatically determined to recover their sacred jewels and to avenge the profanation of their temple by murdering the expedition members and punishing the whole city from which they came.

To bolster this romantic theory, they printed interviews with survivors of the Carnegie Hall and Doyer Street Mission tragedies who recounted the story of the amazing appearance of the Blazing Eye. And, finally, there were statements from internes and doctors who had treated the victims and confessed that they could ascribe the strange deaths to no rational cause—to nothing known to medical science.

A curse *had* descended upon New York, Wentworth admitted, but that curse was entirely human; a monster or monsters of mortal flesh and blood. By what eerie means their seemingly supernatural deviltry was accomplished, he did not know—but already their purpose was all too plain to him. Somewhere behind this rapidly mounting terror lurked an unscrupulous fiend who cold-bloodedly plotted to make capital of the suffering and death he caused; plotted to shackle the city in chains of terror that would enslave the rich and the poor!

As he skimmed through the editions another news account leaped out of the page and caught his attention—another little incident that revealed the slimy trail of the monster that was fastening his foul grip upon the city.

"Patrolman John Gunther, passing on his rounds beneath the Brooklyn Bridge at about one-thirty this morning," the account read, "heard a thumping and pounding in one of the large wooden sheds used by the Bridge Department employees to store their tools. Thinking that someone had been locked inside accidentally, Gunther forced the door, and was amazed to see four men come staggering out. They were able to walk only a few feet when they collapsed and lay writhing in great agony.

"Apparently they were derelicts who had broken into the shed to huddle together inside for warmth, but when he released them they were dripping with perspiration and babbling incoherently about eyes that had been staring at them in the dark. All four were suffering from a raging fever that was so intense that they seemed to wither before his eyes.

"Gunther put in a call for an ambulance, but before it arrived the men, become inarticulate, had shrunk to mere skeletons. The intense heat which consumed the bodies finally became so great that their smoldering clothing caught fire and burned to ashes on the smoldering skeletons that were all that remained of their bodies.

"When the Memorial Hospital ambulance arrived Gunther was in a dazed condition, suffering from nervous shock. He was taken back to the hospital and committed for observation."

The Blazing Eye—it was at work all over the city! In Carnegie Hall, in the Doyer Street Mission, in Peter Ellison's apartment, in this storehouse shack under the bridge—and God only knew in how many other places that had not come to public attention.

There was something incredibly fiendish at work in the city, something that beaded his brow with cold perspiration when he envisioned its possibilities. Something with which Nick Penozzi, Ansel Alden, Morton Cramer and an amazing conglomeration of Orientals were in some way implicated.

Of the ten white members of the Alden-Harmon Expedition, now only three were alive. Kirkpatrick had provided police guards for them and for the Harmons; that should afford them at least some measure of protection—protection at least against raids such as had resulted in Millar's death. Wentworth doubted that he would be able to wring any further information from any of them. Nick Penozzi still seemed to be his best lead.

After leaving the Doyer Street horror, the night before, he had tried to locate the gang chief; had inquired for him in all his usual haunts—but Penozzi was not to be found. But this morning he ought to be at home; or, if he was out, his apartment might prove even more informative than he.

PENOZZI LIVED in a modern apartment building a block off Stuyvesant Square, where he had a ground-floor suite which afforded him convenient access to the rear court when departure by that route seemed more advisable than by the front. Wentworth reconnoitered the place carefully—and a way of getting into the apartment soon suggested itself.

The building was supplied with maid service. As he watched, he saw a half a dozen of the maids, middle-aged women who wore a light-blue cotton costume, come up from the basement by the service elevator. In one of those outfits he would be admitted to Penozzi's rooms without question—or could pick the lock without danger of interference.

A nearby Third Avenue costuming establishment quickly yielded a woman's gray wig. The housekeeper, he ascertained, was alone in the basement supply room. An urgent telephone call sent her scurrying to one of the top-floor apartments—and he had the room to himself.

Before she returned from her fruitless errand he was clad in a maid's outfit, his face made up to carry off the part, a carpet sweeper, mop and pail under his arm as he stepped out into the corridor that led to Penozzi's suite. Fortunately there were no other maids in that hallway to question him. So far, so good. Now would come the test.

Pushing his finger against the buzzer, he fumbled at the lock with his skeleton key—but the door opened before he had it unlocked. A man stood in the doorway, then backed away as Wentworth stooped to lift the pail and other cleaning implements. He stepped inside, turned to close the door—and suddenly was overwhelmed by men who leaped at him from every side. Four of them he counted as he went down, trying desperately to get at his guns, four of Penozzi's thugs. They pinned him down helplessly and held him there while a fifth man, whom Wentworth recognized as Carlo, Nick's brother, stood above him and glared down at him savagely.

Flat on his back, with an automatic muzzle within a foot of his face, Wentworth could do nothing while they ripped off his wig and maid's costume and yanked his automatics from their shoulder holsters.

"So, Mr. Spider, you go in for cleaning, too," Carlo Penozzi lashed out at him. "That's the way you tricked Nick into letting you in." His dark eyes gleamed with a hatred that was almost maniacal. "All right—you want to clean up. Come in!"

He turned on his heel and started toward the living room, and Wentworth was yanked to his feet. The thugs dragged him through the living room and to a large bedroom beyond. There they released him—but instead of their hands now it was five automatic muzzles that held him fast; five snarling faces watched him wolfishly, and five fingers grimly tightened on triggers

The moment Wentworth glanced into that bedroom he knew that death was very close to him. Death had been there—had left nothing but a charred skeleton stretched on Nick Penozzi's bed; and death was still there, licking its bloodless lips in anticipation of another helpless victim.

That ghastly horror lying on the blackened spring was Nick Penozzi, and these men thought that his shocking death was the work of the Spider—thought that he was the Spider, returned to gloat over his victim! The only reason he was not riddled with lead at that moment was because they deemed shooting too easy, too merciful, a death for him....

Never had Richard Wentworth been in a tighter spot. These men did not know who he was; the name Richard Wentworth would have meant little or nothing to them. They recognized him only as a man of wealth and breeding—and as the Spider, who had warred upon them and murdered their leader. Even before he entered that apartment he had been tried and convicted; sentence had been passed upon him—and now was to be carried out

"The Spider—an uptown big shot!" Carlo Penozzi sneered.

"But when it comes to the do-re-mi, you're after it the same as the rest of us, ain't you? The fifty grand for those sparklers was too much for you to pass up, wasn't it? Well, this time you're not getting away with your bloody killing and spider-stamping—"

"I suppose it's useless to try to defend myself," Wentworth interrupted quietly, as he strove desperately to keep his voice cool and convincing. "You fellows think you know all the answers—but I don't. I don't know anything about the Spider. I have never been in this apartment—"

"That's why you sneak in, in a maid's get-up," Carlo baited.

"I used that expedient simply because I wanted to have a talk with Nick, and because I could reach him in no other way," Wentworth put every bit of his personal magnetism, his natural gifts for salesmanship and leadership, into his words. "I was interested in those temple rubies, yes, I wanted to get together with Nick about them—"

"I'll say you were interested, you rat!" Carlo snarled, and the knuckle of his trigger finger whitened. "You thought he had them and so you roasted him alive! I only wish to hell we had a furnace—"

"If I had killed Nick and left him—like that—what reason would I have had for coming back here to this apartment?" Wentworth turned desperately to the others, addressing himself particularly to one of them who seemed to hesitate, to waver. "What reason would I have had for coming back and sticking my head into a trap like this?"

"You came back to search the place," Carlo flung at him.

"There would have been plenty of time for that while Nick

was dying," Wentworth countered. "Only a fool would come back hours afterward. I tell you I know nothing about this. Maybe the Spider did it; maybe these Tibetan priests the newspapers are talking about. If you kill me, you will be letting the skunk who put Nick through hell get away with it."

It was touch and go at that moment. A hair's breadth more of contraction on Penozzi's trigger, and lead would blast through Wentworth's heart. Touch and go—but the earnest conviction of his tone had its effect. The wavering man nodded his head.

"Maybe he's puttin' it straight, Carlo," he muttered—and Wentworth noticed that his gun muzzle began to lower. "Only a damn fool would come back here—and those Chinks hopped us before. Maybe they come sneaking around last night and got Nick. What was done to him looks like their dirty, heathen killing."

Two of the others nodded their heads in agreement, and even Carlo Penozzi's eyes became less deadly. Reluctant doubt was mirrored in them—and Wentworth took swift advantage of it.

"I think I know how to contact that Oriental outfit," he offered. "That was why I wanted to see Nick."

"You know that?" Carlo leaned forward, His face became livid, and a torrent of curses poured from his lips. "Let me get my hands on their yellow necks and we'll find out quick enough what they know about this!"

In the surge of rage that convulsed him he had lowered his gun. For an instant his eyes flashed to the charred thing that had been his brother, and when he looked back Wentworth was holding his coat open with his right hand, was reaching into the inside pocket with his left.

"I have something here—" he was saying; but suddenly his left hand whipped out and caught Carlo full in the face with a backhand blow.

With the same motion he leaped, the fingers of his right hand closed on Penozzi's gun and wrested it from his hand, and the weapon was roaring as he flung himself into a crouch at the foot of the bed. That bit of legerdemain happened so swiftly that the thugs were left gaping and wide-eyed. Wentworth's first bullet knocked the gun out of the hand of one of them; the next drilled another through the arm just as he was about to go into action. Then it was weaving back and forth in a narrow arc that covered both of the others. Even before he spat the crisp command, the guns were dropping from their fingers.

Quickly Wentworth gathered up the guns and herded the gangsters to the far side of the room. At the doorway he stopped and interrupted Carlo's futile cursing.

"I had nothing to do with what happened to Nick," he repeated. "I do not fight with fire and torture—and neither does the Spider."

Then he was through the doorway, down the corridor and out into the street, where he hailed a passing taxi and told the driver to head for uptown.

SO THERE was truth to the seemingly fantastic story of the temple image's stolen eyes… Sufficient truth, at any rate, to have set one of New York's most powerful gangs on the trail of the gems. That might also explain the visit of those Orientals to Raymond Millar's apartment; might explain Nick Penozzi's ghastly death—murdered by the Orientals, who had trailed his gangsters to his apartment.

In some way, Wentworth was convinced, all of these Blazing Eye deaths were tied up with the doings of the Alden-Harmon Expedition. While refusing to put any faith in the idea of a curse, he nevertheless was willing to believe that the orgy of murder was directly due to something the explorers might have done in Asia or might have brought back.

The jewel image eyes?

Perhaps. More than ever, he wanted to know the truth about that expedition; wanted to know the secrets he was certain the members had not confided to Stanley Kirkpatrick. But where could he get that?

Not from Morton Cramer—that was fairly certain. Cramer already had demonstrated his capacity for evasion, his intention of keeping to himself whatever he knew. And not from Ansel Alden—that was absolutely certain. Alden was not the revealing sort; anything which he knew would remain locked in his brain until he had occasion to reveal it—at a profit to himself. That left only James Kennedy....

Wentworth leaned forward and gave the driver the address of the club at which the aerial navigator was staying.

Kennedy was there when he arrived, and immediately it was apparent that he was more than glad of the visit. Some of the man's self-confidence was gone. There were shadows under his eyes, lines of worry in his brow; and even as he welcomed Went-

worth his eyes probed the big reception room of the famous club, uneasily.

"I think perhaps it might be better if we go up to my room," he suggested. "We can talk more freely there."

Wentworth's first bullet knocked the gun out of the hand of one thug—the next drilled another through the arm.

Wentworth noticed that he locked the door of the bedroom after them, but as soon as they were alone inside his uneasiness seemed to abate.

"Nothing has happened to the others?" he asked anxiously; and then, when Wentworth had reassured him, "I suppose I am unduly nervous—but when seven out of ten of us have died...."

"There is something more than that which makes you uneasy, Kennedy," Wentworth plumped at him. "Something that happened out there in Asia, probably. You know what it is—and you may save your own life by divulging it. Ellison and Millar called on me for help when it was too late. There is still time for you to come clean."

It was plain that Kennedy welcomed the opportunity to unburden himself.

"We did loot a native temple," he admitted nervously. "That day when Ellison's plane took the side trip to Kur-ogan. It was really a sort of shrine where the Mongols had a big statue of Genghis Khan. The thing must have been ten feet high, and the eyes were two of the largest, finest rubies I ever saw. We had the place to ourselves for a few minutes and managed to get one of them pried loose before the old lama who had charge of the place came back inside.

"The idea was Morton Cramer's. He had heard of this shrine and wanted to have a try at the stones. He took charge of the one we nabbed and was to dispose of it when we got to New York, and then divide up with the rest of us—just the five who were on the plane, not the others."

Genghis Khan! That was the name Moo Fong had spelled out

with the lids of his blinded eyes. His dying warning had been something about Genghis Khan destroying the city....

"All our trouble started from the time we took that eye," Kennedy was saying. "We—"

Suddenly the lights went out, and his voice ended in a gasp of fright. For an instant the room seemed to be utterly black—and then Wentworth saw that there was a dim illumination.

"The eye!" Kennedy screamed in wild terror. "There it is!"

Wentworth whirled—and stared up at a blazing eye, fully six inches wide, that glared down at him from the wall! An eye that seemed to burn with a cold, uncanny light!

One look he took, and then he threw himself flat on the floor and started crawling toward the door.

"Down, Kennedy—down!" he shouted; but Kennedy seemed transfixed, utterly fascinated by the doom that confronted him.

On his belly Wentworth wriggled to the door and reached up his hand to turn the key in the lock. Tugging it open, he fairly catapulted himself out into the hallway and then pushed the door wide so that Kennedy could follow. But already that was too late. Kennedy had dropped to the floor and lay there groaning and writhing in terrible agony.

"The eye—the eye!" he moaned. "It's got me, Wentworth. All hell is raging in my insides. I'm burning up! *Oh-h-h—*"

His voice ended in a gasping sob as he doubled up with pain and threshed wildly—but by then Wentworth had managed to reach him. On hands and knees he had dared to edge his way into the room until he could reach the sufferer and drag him out into the hall.

WHAT HE beheld when the light fell on Kennedy's figure shocked him. Already the navigator's body was withered and shrunken—not more than half its normal size, it seemed. His face was bathed with perspiration that rolled off him in streams, and his flesh was so hot that to touch it was like placing a hand on a hot stove. Running down the hall to the bathroom, Wentworth came back with a glass of water, but Kennedy could not swallow it. The liquid would go no farther than his throat—and it actually seemed to turn to steam in his mouth!

Now he could no longer speak; could only writhe horribly—and shrink away like a waxen figure thrust into a roaring fire. Helpless, Wentworth could only watch while his body was consumed in an incredibly short time; burned to a crisp by the fearful inferno that raged within him. Seared by terrible inner fires until the terrific heat set his smoldering clothing on fire—until the shrunken flesh that clung to the bones after the clothing fell away became incandescent and then burned out to a black char....

Wentworth felt that he was watching the working of hell during those awful minutes. He was transfixed by horror—but at last he shook off the numbing coma and ran back to the door of Kennedy's room, to turn his pocket-flash into it. When the light fell on that blazing eye it disappeared from the wall—which was just what he expected. The thing was painted there on the wall with phosphorous. But there must be something more to it than that.

There was! Creeping up beneath the eye, he examined it more closely—and saw that there was a metallic body to the phosphorescent paint. That was it! A metallic body that must have acted as a magnet for whatever killed Kennedy; a magnet that attracted a current or a ray that was utterly fiendish in its inception!

And that death-dealing device must have been behind Kennedy, on the other side of the room, near the window.

Flat on his stomach, Wentworth started toward the far side, but before he had negotiated more than a third of the distance the room shook beneath a deafening explosion, and a whole section of the wall he had intended to inspect was blown to pieces. Too late now; Wentworth got to his feet and shook off the pulverized plaster that covered him. The answer to Kennedy's death and to the horror of the Blazing Eye had been almost within reach of his hand, but now it had been blown to atoms by that roaring blast!

The crash of the explosion brought men running upstairs from the club rooms below, but before they arrived Wentworth had discovered a well-hidden dictograph in the wreckage, its wires torn away by the destroying blast so that there was no chance of tracing it. What had happened was plain. Somewhere, perhaps close by, someone had sat listening to every word of Kennedy's conversation and had switched on the death machine when the moment came to silence him.

But who was that hidden listener? Ansel Alden? Morton Cramer? Wentworth had no way of telling, but he intended to find out—and that without delay. The time had come when both Alden and Cramer must talk, whether they wanted to or not.

Both must be covered at once, must be watched every moment, and to do that he would need assistance.

While he was waiting for the police to arrive, he went to the telephone to call Sutton Place and enlist the aid of Jackson, his chauffeur and capable right-hand man—but to his amazement there was no answer. No answer on his regular line or on the special, unlisted lines he used in cases of emergency.

Wentworth was worried at once. No answer to those calls meant serious trouble, for one of the strictest rules of the Sutton Place establishment was that at all times either Jenkyns, Jackson or Ram Singh, Wentworth's faithful Sikh personal man, must be on hand, ready to answer the telephone, when he was not at home....

It seemed ages before the police arrived and finished their questioning. The moment they released him on his own recognizance he hurried out to the taxi that stood waiting and sped across town.

Carefully he entered his stronghold, using the dummy apartment on Sutton Place and the underground passageway that led to the building in the rear. Gun in hand, he stepped warily out of the elevator on the third floor. All was quiet there. Not a sound as he stepped from the foyer into his living room—and then his hair seemed to rise and stand straight on end!

There, in the middle of the familiar room, was a tableau that froze the blood.

On the floor, securely bound and gagged, lay Jackson, Jenkyns and the tall bearded Sikh—but it was at his own favorite easy chair that Wentworth stared. Now it had a ghastly occupant.

Propped up on the cushions was the dead body of Morton Cramer—Morton Cramer with two huge, gleaming red stones that looked like rubies jammed into the blood-dripping sockets of his gouged-out eyes!

CHAPTER 5
DEAD LIPS SPEAK

EXCEPT FOR minor, superficial bruises, the others were unharmed, but they had been so ingeniously tied together that they could make no attempt to free themselves without choking one another. Helplessly they lay there until Wentworth untied them—and loosed the flood of explanations that poured from their lips.

"It was about two and a half hours ago when Mr. Cramer telephoned the first time," Jackson outlined what had happened. "He seemed very anxious to reach you; so much so that he called again about thirty minutes later and begged me to get in touch with you somehow. That time he seemed to be so terrified that I suggested he might come here and wait for you to return. He accepted that invitation eagerly; said he would be over immediately—and he was, not more than fifteen minutes later.

"I heard his horn outside and went to open the gates for him, but before I could lead the way back into the house four men pounced upon us. Two Chinese and two Japanese, they appeared to be. They had been hiding in the grounds and leaped out from concealment the moment my back was turned. I should have seen them, sir, I realize that—but I had not the slightest suspicion that anyone would be there, inside the wall—"

He halted.

"That is the least part of it, *sahib.*" Ram Singh's dark, bearded face was abject, his turbaned head bowed in shame. "Four of them overcame Jackson and Mr. Cramer—but only two were needed to dispose of thy servant and Jenkyns. As soon as Jackson left the building they must have slipped through the door—and after that they had only to creep up and hit this helpless one over the head. When I again knew what was happening they had tied me as you found me. It would have been better had the gun barrel gone through my skull and saved me this disgrace."

Ram Singh's deep, nasal voice was filled with contrition. The son of a long line of Indian warriors, he had bent the knee to no man until he met Wentworth, the one whom he was proud to call master. Since that time he had served his white lord with a devotion and dependability that would permit of no mistakes.

"There is no such thing as perfection, my warrior," Wentworth tried to ease his mortification. "The best of men err. What sort of men were these who overcame you and Jenkyns?"

"One was a Chinese, master," Ram Singh replied. "The other appeared to be more like a Mongolian, or perhaps an inhabitant of Tibet. They were upon us so quickly that there was little time for observation. After they had gone and there was time to think, it came to me that all six of them must have climbed to the roof of the building on Sutton Place and then lowered themselves into our grounds, to wait there for the arrival of Mr.

Cramer. That is a possibility against which it would be well to take precautions in the future."

"Cramer knew that he was doomed the moment he saw them," Jackson resumed the account. "He was terrified when he arrived, but after that he lost all hope, just gave up. They dragged us all up here and then tried to make him talk. They asked him a lot of questions about where he had hidden something, but he just stared at them without answering a word—until they put those two big stones on the table. Then he knew the end had come.

"He made a desperate effort to break away, but they held him tightly and jabbed a knife into his eyes—and then stuck the stones there where you see them. Even then, Cramer shouted something to us in Hindustani, but before he could finish they fell on him and stabbed him to death."

"The message was for you, *sahib*," Ram Singh supplemented. "He said to look in a safe-deposit box that is in your name in the Times Square branch of the Chemical National Bank."

A safe-deposit box—that would be available until three o'clock. Wentworth glanced at his watch. It was two-fifteen. Still time to reach the bank before the closing hour—though what he would do with the stolen eye of Genghis Khan was more than he knew. Perhaps, if he got possession of it, he could contact its rightful owners and put an end to this orgy of murder....

Wentworth lost no time hurrying from the apartment and speeding across town to the bank in a taxi, but when he was admitted to the safe-deposit vault and opened the little metal box that was placed before him a surprise awaited him. There was no gem in the receptacle. Instead, there was a typewritten statement addressed to him—a statement signed by Morton Cramer.

"When you read this, the fact that you are doing so will be sufficient evidence that I have been double-crossed," Cramer's dead voice seemed to speak to him from the typed page. "It will mean that I have paid with my life for mixing with something that I ought to have kept my hands off.

"By this time, you may know that while we were in Kur-ogan we looted a native shrine and stole one of the eyes out of a statue enthroned there. I had been commissioned to get both those eyes but could pry only one loose before the native priests interrupted us. It was so that I could secure these gems that our route was laid out to include Sachi-buluk.

"When Thompson, Hardy, Newsome and Powell died, I believed that we had been followed from Kur-ogan to America and that Orientals on this side of the Pacific took up the chase when we arrived in San Francisco. To try to get rid of them, I had very convincing imitations of the gem made. One of these I hid in Ellison's apartment, another in Millar's, hoping that one of them would be found if the apartments were raided and searched and that the Orientals would think it was the original and be satisfied to return with it to Asia.

"But that plan failed. I knew that when the Orientals who had found the imitation gem in Ellison's apartment were not satisfied with it and went on to Millar's. After that I knew that my own life was in constant jeopardy. I had been assured of protection—but your reading of this statement will prove that the promise was not kept. Now I know that it will prove, also, that I and the other members of the expedition were deliberately murdered to close our mouths and eliminate us.

"The genuine gem is hidden in the prayer wheel—"

That was as far as Wentworth got. Suddenly he realized that the air in the vault was very stuffy. He felt his senses reeling, began to choke—and toppled over just as he knew that the vault was filling with gas.

THAT WAS the last thing he remembered until he came back to his senses and found himself lying on the floor. The metal box was on the table where he had left it, but the statement was gone—and then he knew that the Orientals who had murdered Morton Cramer must have understood his Hindustani message to Ram Singh!

Back into Wentworth's seething mind came the words of that last sentence he had half-finished reading. "The genuine gem is hidden in the prayer wheel—" The prayer wheel—that was in Nita's apartment! The prayer wheel Fred Powell had brought from Tibet for her! Cramer had devilishly chosen it as a hiding-place for the stolen ruby—and now the Orientals knew about his trick!

Wentworth groaned inwardly as he envisioned what had happened the moment they read that statement. They would lose no time going to her apartment—would have reached there before now....

The police had drawn a cordon around the bank and would permit nobody to leave, but at last Wentworth persuaded them to allow him to use the telephone. He called Nita's apartment—

and there was no answer. Those fiends had reached her!

Frenziedly he tried to get out of the bank, but the police lieutenant in charge was adamant. Precious minutes slipped by, and it was not until Wentworth was able to contact Stanley Kirkpatrick that he was released.

Grisly fear rode him as a taxi sped him toward Riverside Drive and Nita's apartment; horrible fear of what he would find when he reached there.

At last the taxi reached the Riverside Towers and he leaped out. On the run he started for

ANSEL ALDEN

RAY MILLAR

CARLO PENOZZI

JAMES KENNEDY

VIOLA DUNN

TRUEMAN HARMON

the doorway, but subconsciously he noticed a car starting away from the curb just beyond it—a car from which a familiar face peered out at him. Viola Dunn! He placed her as he sped across the lobby and into an elevator that started upstairs immediately.

Viola Dunn in a car outside Riverside Towers… But there was no time to mull over that now. Wentworth dismissed the girl from his thoughts as he reached Nita's floor and sprinted toward her door.

There was no answer to his ring; but he already had his key in his hand, had it in the lock, turning. Warily he opened the door—and then leaped, crouching with gun ready, to one side of the foyer. The apartment was empty, but there had been somebody there very recently. A window was wide open, and the place had the indefinable feel of occupancy, the feel of a place from which human beings had just departed.

Swiftly Wentworth searched the rooms. There was no sign of Nita—and for that he breathed a sigh of relief. Far better to find her gone than to discover another ghastly horror stretched out on a blackened bedspring. That, he felt certain, would have shaken his sanity....

Nita was gone, but very evidently she had not gone without a struggle. The apartment was upset from end to end. It had been ransacked, and furniture was tumbled in every direction. Wentworth's probing eyes searched carefully—and when he righted an upset end table he found what he sought. The prayer wheel! It had been smashed to bits, its hub split in two with a knife. The ruby, if it had been hidden there, was gone.

But if the raiders had recovered their gem, why had they taken Nita with them? For some devilish purpose of torture? Some outlandish idea of propitiating the outraged image in their profaned temple?

He paced the apartment, desperately seeking some clue that might tell him where they had taken her; some little sign that she might have left to lead him after her... There was nothing... nothing but a note which was lying in the center of her writing desk. It had been written on her own typewriter.

Wentworth picked it up and read it through; stared at it and tried to understand what lay behind its cryptic message.

"I also arrived too late to find the jewels or Miss van Sloan," it mocked him, "but a word to the wise should be sufficient. Trueman Harmon is an avid and reputedly unscrupulous gem collector—and he also has a decided weakness for lovely women."

There was no signature, but none was necessary. Wentworth was certain that Ansel Alden had written that note—just as certain as if he had watched him type it. Ansel Alden had written it—but why?

The explorer would answer that question himself, Wentworth resolved grimly, but first he had to call Kirkpatrick. He had promised to let the commissioner know what he discovered at Nita's apartment. Twice he dialed the number, but Kirkpatrick's line was busy—and then he had left the office for an indefinite period....

WHEN STANLEY KIRKPATRICK put down the telephone, after Wentworth had called him from the Chemical National Bank, he sat and stared across his office for long minutes. More Oriental deviltry! It seemed to be hemming him in on every side. Murders, suicides, extortion demands, appeals for help from frantic victims—there had been far more of it than he had admitted to Wentworth in their few minutes' conversation outside the house in which the blackened remains of Chris Randall lay stretched on a bedspring.

Even then the Blazing Eye had become a bugaboo to him. He had seen nearly a dozen of those rice-paper warnings that burst into flame the moment they came in contact with moisture; had talked with twice that number of businessmen who were resisting demands for contributions to various funds which were no more than extortion rackets. Every time his telephone rang he expected to hear of another threat, death, or outrage that would shock the city.

And now they had had the temerity to invade a bank and gas the whole safe-deposit vault—and that in the heart of Times Square!

Tiring of their sensational Asiatic curse stories, the newspapers were beginning to protest against this unchecked reign of terror, and Kirkpatrick could already hear what they would have to say about this brazen attack on a bank in the heart of the city. But his gloomy meditation was interrupted by the announcement that Mr. John Wenzel, who had called half an hour ago, was outside waiting to see him.

John Wenzel was the partner of Henry Mung. Between them, they operated the largest string of chop suey restaurants in the city. Wenzel had been afraid to state his business over the telephone, but his anxious voice and blustering excitement had told their own story. Kirkpatrick knew just about what he was going to hear, even before his office door opened to admit the heavy, thickset, slightly paunchy German-American.

"I have come to you for protection, Commissioner," Wenzel blurted even before he had settled into the chair beside Kirkpatrick's desk. "That's something new for me. I fight my own battles and take care of myself—but now, with what has been going on in this city, I am afraid for my customers. I can't take chances with such murderers. That's why I want help. I want policemen for all my places—plainclothesmen so that my customers won't know they are there."

"Begin at the beginning, Wenzel," Kirkpatrick cut through the excited rush of words. "Why do you want protection? What happened?"

"Four days ago," Wenzel made a determined effort to be calm, "we got the first call. A Chinese feller came to my office and told me that we were put down for a contribution to the All-Eastern Fund. Two thousand dollars contribution he wanted!—not from us; from *each one* of our restaurants; and we have twenty-six!

"What would you do with a feller like that? I threw him out— but after he was gone I noticed that Henry Mung looked scared. He wouldn't say much when I asked him what was the matter; but I got him to admit that he never heard of this All-Eastern Fund. That was all for then, but two days later somebody called me on the phone and told me we had just two more days to make our contribution to the fund. He hung up when I started to tell him what I thought of him and his gang.

"Today is the second day—and this morning we got this." Out of his pocket he took an envelope from which he gingerly spilled one of the Blazing Eye's death warnings. "Henry Mung, he wanted me to pay. He tried to stop me from coming to you— but I don't pay a penny to racketeers." Wenzel's jaw squared belligerently and his fists clenched. "I licked Hymie Shapiro's gang when they tried to hold me up—and no bunch of Chinks are gonna scare me with their trick warnings.

"I want protection, Commissioner. I want you should put men

in our places right away—tonight. There's no telling how soon these devils might try some of their funny work—"

Again the telephone rang, and Kirkpatrick reached for it with some annoyance—but instantly he was all attention.

"This is Doctor Leon De Santo," a crisp, troubled voice announced; "Mr. Henry Mung's physician. Mr. Mung called me ten minutes ago, but by the time I reached him he was delirious—stricken with this peculiar malady that has invaded the city. I can make out very little of what he says—but there is something about an eye that is staring at him and something about calling you and John Wenzel."

"Can you do anything for him, Doctor?" Kirkpatrick asked—even though he knew what the answer would be.

"I have never seen anything like it," the physician's voice was puzzled, baffled. "His body is being consumed by a terrific fever that is wasting it away. I have already sent out a call for specialists—but I am afraid they will be as helpless as I am. This isn't a case for doctors, Commissioner. It isn't sickness—it is outright murder!"

Cold-blooded murder—deliberately perpetrated to serve as a lesson to any who might be tempted to go to the police when it was their turn to contribute to the "All-Eastern Fund"! In that moment Kirkpatrick knew that he was faced with the worst extortion plot of his experience—a brazen scheme to trade on an unholy terror that was far more appalling than even the threat of death. Already that terror was spreading through the city, sowing the seeds for wild, unreasoning panic....

"Something has happened—something has happened to

Mung?" Wenzel's anxious, intuitive question brought him back to the immediate present.

"Henry Mung will be dead before you can get back to him," Kirkpatrick told him gently. "He must have been stricken right after you left to come here"

"Yes—right after I left," Wenzel mumbled. "I killed him—I killed him. He didn't want me to come—he said we couldn't fight this thing—said it was too big for us…too big for anybody"

As he spoke he leaned forward on the desk, and his face became pasty-white, beaded with perspiration. Kirkpatrick stared at that face in terrible fascination—stared at the man's forehead, where something was beginning to appear. Something that became a livid, almond-shaped eye—the mark of John Wenzel's doom!

CHAPTER 6
CHAPEL OF THE EYE

UNABLE TO reach Stanley Kirkpatrick by telephone, Wentworth left word of Nita's kidnapping for the commissioner and then set out to find Ansel Alden. First at his hotel, then at the Explorers Club, and from there to four other places where men at the club thought he might be—but Alden was in none of them. He had disappeared; had eluded the police guard the commissioner had assigned to him and had not been seen all day.

That did not surprise Wentworth; it fitted in perfectly with the role he had been constructing for the explorer.

Alden, he reasoned, had learned of the looting of the Kur-ogan temple even though the crew of the second plane had told him nothing about their depredation. Supposing that Cramer and his mates had stolen both eyes from the image, he was convinced that the gems were of great value. That was a bitter pill for a man who was accustomed to taking for himself the lion's share of the credit and profit from every expedition with which he was connected—so bitter that he had enlisted the aid of Nick Penozzi to try to locate the hiding-place of the gems.

Nick had paid with his life for his efforts, but no doubt his brother was carrying on in his stead. And no doubt Carlo would know where to get in touch with Alden....

For Wentworth to try to locate Carlo Penozzi in his own guise would have been worse than useless; would have been suicidal. The moment that Carlo or any of the four companions who were with him that morning in Nick's apartment saw the man who had tricked them so neatly they would reach for their guns—or their knives. Before he could explain his intentions he would have to kill them.

But where Richard Wentworth was bound to fail, Blinky McQuade would succeed, for Blinky was well known to the Penozzi gang and hundreds of other denizens of the under-world.

It was so that Wentworth might have access to the closely guarded haunts of gangland that Blinky McQuade had come into being. An ex-safecracker and a penitentiary graduate he had admitted he was, when he made his appearance in the dingiest part of the slums. Frowsy and weak-eyed, a has-been hang-er-on at the criminal fringe, the lords of the underworld had accepted him with a shrug; had tolerated him because he was too insignificant to be worth their notice. The third identity of Richard Wentworth's triple personality, it was Blinky McQuade who secured many of the tips and leads that served the Spider so well—and it was to Blinky that Wentworth turned now as a taxi bore him deep into that maze of narrow, congested and evil-smelling streets that lies to the east of the Bowery.

Several blocks from his destination he dismissed the cab, to penetrate on foot the rest of the labyrinthian way to the V-point where dismal, squalor-drenched Holian Alley joins with equally uninviting Pallin Place. Down Pallin Place he walked, to step into the unlocked doorway of Number 2, pass through the dank-smelling hallway to the tiny communal courtyard behind it and then enter the rear door of Number 1 "Holy Alley." Up the creaking, foot-worn stairs to the second floor he picked his way, to unlock the door of a dingy, poorly furnished back room.

The huge bed which took up most of that room was its only decent-looking article of furniture. Wentworth made prompt use of it. Kneeling on the quilts, he pressed certain spots on the imposing, ornate headboard, and a section of it opened outward like a desk, to provide him with a fully equipped make-up table.

In front of the lighted mirror he went to work, and again his skilled fingers performed a miracle of transformation. Into his mouth went a prepared pad that made his lower lip pendulous and lax. Lotion applied to his cheeks made his skin sallow and taut across the cheekbones, ready for the dark, heavily shadowed lines of age he painted in adeptly. A streaking of gray in his rumpled hair—and the immaculate Richard Wentworth had disappeared completely.

When he had donned a soiled shirt and a ragged suit of clothing and had added a pair of thick-lensed, metal-hooded glasses, Blinky McQuade was ready to shamble out into the only world that knew him. Round-shouldered and short-sighted, he pushed his way through the noisy, crowded, rubbish-littered streets, glowering sourly whenever anyone got in his way. To one who watched him pass he would have seemed half-blind, but behind those powerful-lensed spectacles his eyes, reputedly weak and almost useless during the daytime, missed nothing that went on around him.

One after the other, he dropped in at three bars and two poolrooms, shuffled upstairs to a "smoke joint," had a sandwich and a cup of coffee in a restaurant that was actually a clearinghouse for criminals passing through the city. And from the very first of the resorts he entered his acute senses detected something unnatural, something that was indefinably changed.

FOR SOME time he tried to put his finger on just what it was. These places seemed quieter, more subdued, more secretive than he had ever known them to be. Not only were there fewer loungers on hand than usual—but those who were there kept more to themselves; and when he did catch their eyes or engage them in small talk he readily sensed a suppressed excitement, a half-fear, about them that was unmistakable.

It eluded his every attempt to identify it until he climbed the stairs to the second-floor quarters of Balmy's Bit House. The broken-nosed ex-pugilist was behind his almost-deserted bar and was more than glad to lean on his elbow at Blinky's end of it.

"What's come over this goofy town?" Blinky growled as he poured himself a drink of Balmy's best whisky. "Come back after a few weeks and the whole damn place seems changed. Everybody acts like they're afraid to crack their faces by grinning. Looks like they had an election and voted in the reform ticket."

Balmy contemplated the deserted booths that lined the opposite wall and spat in disgust.

"Worse'n that," he grunted. "You can handle a reform administration—but how in hell can you handle religion? Never thought I'd see the day when these roughnecks would fall for anything like that—but it's come, by Jeez. They've all gone nuts!"

Religion! Wentworth barely repressed a gasp of amazement, but before he could question Balmy farther several other customers came in and the proprietor was kept busy. The underworld had gone for religion… That was all the clue Blinky needed. To have shown more interest by resuming the subject there in the Bit House would have been out of character for the grumpy, uncommunicative individual his acquaintances knew him to be—but already he had picked out the person who would know all about this sudden wave of religion.

Deacon Baumgarten!

The Deacon was a suave, unctuous individual who admitted to being an unfrocked clergyman. Always ready with a soft-spoken homily, he could pick a pocket with a prayer on his lips. Several times he had attempted to organize cults of his own but had been discouraged when the police raided him and threatened him with prison for his unorthodox methods of finance. For Blinky McQuade he held a soft spot in his heart, principally because the frowsy cracksman could generally be cajoled into buying several drinks of first-rate cognac.

Blinky located the tall, thin, solemn-faced Deacon in the rear of a "coffee pot" where his favorite beverage was dispensed without the formality of revenue stamps. After the third drink he became not only loquacious but evangelistic.

"We are on the eve of a new day, Blinky," he warmed to his subject. "A new day that will see the emancipation of all mankind. Poverty and prisons will be a thing of the past. Under a new leader the united world will be reinspired, reorganized, rejuvenated. The good work is well under way. You can already witness its effects all around you—and that is the result of only our first chapel!"

With the fourth brandy clutched in his long fingers he eyed Blinky speculatively—and the missionary zeal was upon him.

"You should be one of us, McQuade," he beamed. "Now is the time to affiliate, when the movement is young and leaders are being chosen." Half-hesitantly he looked at his watch, but the fervor of the converter was stronger than his desire for another drink—which it was doubtful that Blinky would buy, anyway. "I can take you to the chapel now," he decided. "We are late, but the service will still be in progress."

BLINKY SHRUGGED his shoulders but offered no objection. Wordlessly he followed the Deacon several blocks to what had once been a small neighborhood mission. Now the place was reopened—but the moment he stepped inside he saw that its character had been materially changed. Now, instead of the black-garbed, earnest little man who had held forth from its pulpit, the chapel was manned by Chinese, Japanese, Hindus, and several of whose nationality he could not be sure. They were all there. And, framed on the wall behind the low altar, was a picture that riveted his attention the instant he saw it. A life-size picture of a Mongolian conqueror who could be none other than Genghis Khan!

Blinky was ushered to a seat beside the Deacon, but already his quick eyes had swept every corner of that amazing chapel; had cataloged the surprising congregation. The men who crowded the benches were not only the slum-dwellers he expected. Every grade of society seemed to be represented there—Orientals and whites, rich and poor, hard-faced criminals and simple, honest-looking shopkeepers. All seemed to have found a common medium in this outlandish cult....

The service was highly emotional and gripped its devotees firmly. Their eyes gleamed with the fervor of fanaticism, and a soft, ecstatic sigh went up from their lips when the lights dimmed and went out—all except special lights beneath the altar which played upon the picture of Genghis Khan from several angles.

Wentworth stared—and the weird lighting effect fascinated him. As he watched, the figure seemed to come to life; seemed to step right out of its background. Especially the eyes; they blazed out of the round face with hypnotic intensity that cast a spell over the worshipers.

In the absolute silence, the voice of one of who seemed to be the high priest droned a sort of litany.

"Genghis Khan, almighty conqueror of all nations and all races, master of all the world," he chanted. "Thy people have been waiting too long for thy return. The world lies in the hands of unworthy stewards; thy people cry out for relief and for—"

Gradually Wentworth began to realize the significance of what he was hearing and witnessing. These people had accepted the belief that Genghis Khan, the great Mongol conqueror of the Twelfth Century, had returned to earth and was about to pursue his divinely appointed mission to establish a world empire! That was the secret of this strange brotherhood of ordinarily hostile Orientals—a union beneath the banner of the leader who would give them mastery of the world!

Again Wentworth caught the fanatical gleam in the eyes of those around him, and as he listened he caught ominous phrases in their patter. The All-Seeing Eye... The Eye of the World... The Destroying Flame... This devilish cult was directly tied up with the Blazing Eye; was no doubt responsible for the outrages which had shocked the whole city!

And yet, he admitted, there was nothing illegal about this meeting. The police were helpless—but not the Spider! It was for emergencies just such as this that the Nemesis of crime had come into being—and now, more than ever in his tempestuous career, the Spider had an opportunity, an inescapable obligation, to prove his worth!

Amazed and awed by the far-reaching, evil possibilities of that poisonous cult, Wentworth left the meeting with the

Deacon and followed him several blocks without speaking. Then he stopped and was about to go his own way—but Baumgarten grasped his arm and held him.

"Not yet, my friend," he protested. "You were very generous to me a while ago. Now it will be my privilege to repay your hospitality. I am hungry and I know a little place where we can find good food. After we have eaten, it will be time enough for you to go."

Wentworth took care not to betray his surprise, but to have the Deacon offer to repay a treat was unheard-of. There was a reason behind that invitation....

Wentworth shrugged and went along. West toward the Bowery, in the direction of Chinatown, he noticed, the Deacon was leading. It was nearly ten o'clock. The tenement-lined streets were less populated, quieting down for the night—but when they were less than a block away from Chinatown's Pell Street the nocturnal peace was suddenly shattered. Suddenly they were face to face with stark tragedy!

DISTANT SCREAMS signaled that tragedy; then the eerie wail of police sirens and the rush of curious people running to see what had happened. Instinctively Wentworth glanced at the Deacon—and saw at once that he did not have to wonder about the cause of the disturbance; *he knew!* His face gleamed with excitement, and he started on a half-run to the spot where an awed crowd had already gathered.

The wild screams were coming from a large chop suey restaurant on the second floor of a corner building. Most of the big windows had already been smashed out, and the bodies of men and women came plunging through them as Wentworth joined the crowd that kept at a safe distance. Down onto the sidewalk the bodies plummeted, to lie there writhing and squirming, while a hysterical babble came from the lips of the victims.

"The eye—the eye!" Wentworth recognized the ghastly plaint he knew so well. "It's burning into me! I'm on fire inside! God in heaven—help me—*help me!*"

Help them—but nobody could! His blood ran cold as he listened to those pitiful pleas, but there was nothing that he could do. The door and stairway leading to the restaurant were already jammed with customers who fought one another frenziedly in their efforts to escape. No chance of getting upstairs from that direction, and he would have been swept away from the windows even had he been able to reach them.

Helplessly he looked up at that raging bedlam—and then glanced at the building behind him. There was what appeared to be a hall window on the second floor. Stepping into the doorway, he quickly picked the lock and hurried up the stairs to the next landing—and from there he looked right into the pit of hell!

The restaurant across the way had been turned into a panic-ridden madhouse. The lights were out, but an eerie, bluish-white radiance illuminated the big dining room and dance floor, weirdly. Tables and chairs had been overturned, and men and women floundered among them; picked themselves up and were knocked down again by others who fought frantically to reach the choked stairway or the windows.

In the center of the dance floor the Chinese manager was doing his best to calm the fearful turmoil, but nobody paid him the slightest attention. Only one thought was in every mind—to get away from the great, malignantly gleaming, almond-shaped eye that blazed down on the doomed victims. Like a sentient thing, that huge orb, fully two feet in width, seemed to gloat down on their futile struggles.

Wild bedlam—and then came the fire! It sprang up from the floor—from still figures that lay entwined with the tables; withered figures that had wasted away to almost nothing. Instantly it swept the restaurant from end to end. One moment the manager stood there with his hands raised imploringly—and then he was engulfed in the blaze that was all around him.

The Blazing Eye had scored again—and Deacon Baumgarten and the congregation of that devil's chapel had known what was going to happen. That was why the sanctimonious hypocrite had pretended his invitation; he had deliberately led Wentworth there to witness this demonstration of the Blazing Eye's scourging power....

There was nothing Wentworth could do for the victims who leaped out onto the sidewalk; nothing he could do for those still trapped in the restaurant. The blight of that hellish Blazing Eye had doomed them beyond human aid. Physically sick with the realization of his impotence, he went back downstairs into the street and stood there, rooted by horror to the sidewalk.

"Maybe it's just as well Henry Mung didn't live to see this," a fellow-bystander ventured as he stared, wide-eyed, at the tragic scene. "That was his first restaurant—his favorite place."

"Henry Mung?" Wentworth tried to place the name.

"He and John Wenzel owned the place," his informant

explained. "This was their first. Now the string extends all over the city. Mung died this afternoon. I don't know how—but there's a rumor going around that he was murdered because he wouldn't come across to a gang of racketeers. Damn shame, if he was—Mung was a white guy!"

Henry Mung and John Wenzel—now Wentworth placed them; and now he knew why Mung's name had struck a reminiscent chord in his brain. He had heard it that very evening; had heard it mentioned with peculiar emphasis during the chapel service—emphasis that now had new significance. This fearful slaughter of innocent diners was punishment for Henry Mung—even though the man already was dead!

More than that, Wentworth realized, what he was witnessing was intended as a horrible example, as a terrible warning to the whole city, a shocking demonstration of what happened when the demands of the Blazing Eye were not met!

Henry Mung's favorite restaurant… But the chain which he and Wenzel controlled must operate twenty or more throughout New York. Perhaps the others, too, were in danger? Stanley Kirkpatrick must be warned of that possibility, at any rate, so that he could take precautions to protect them.

WENTWORTH HURRIED to a telephone and waited fully ten minutes before he was able to reach the commissioner at headquarters. Then the voice that came to him over the wire was weary and discouraged.

"I know, Dick," Kirkpatrick groaned. "I know about Mung's place in Chinatown—and about twenty-five others, as well. The whole chain of restaurants—all twenty-six of them—were stricken simultaneously. Ten o'clock was the signal for hell to break loose in all of them. There must be over a thousand victims who were caught in the traps!

"Henry Mung?" he echoed Wentworth's question. "He died this afternoon—burned to a skeleton by the Blazing Eye. Since then his partner, John Wenzel, has been trying frantically to get in touch with the murdering devils and pay the extortion money he refused to give them. He has tried everything—even managed to get onto the air before I could prevent him. But nothing succeeded—and tonight you see what happened."

"Where is Wenzel now?" Wentworth wanted to know.

"I have him in a cell here at headquarters," the commissioner answered. "On a charge of virtually holding up the radio station and grabbing their facilities—but I am holding him only in protective custody. His life has been threatened, and in the state he is now he is likely to kill himself if the Eye doesn't get him first. But I fear I shall have to turn him loose. His lawyer is arranging bail for him now."

"I want to have a talk with him before he gets away—it's important, Kirk," Wentworth said quickly. "Hold onto him until I get there, will you? What he knows may tie up with something else I discovered tonight—may give me the lead I need to find Nita."

"I'll stall him if the papers come through before you get here," Kirkpatrick agreed. "But make it snappy."

Wentworth made it snappy. In less than ten minutes he was at the door of the office and Kirkpatrick rose to meet him.

"He's still here," he reassured. "Haven't heard from his lawyer yet. We'll go back to the cells and bring him to the office."

But John Wenzel never returned to the commissioner's office. When they arrived at his cell he was lying on the floor, moaning and writhing in agony, his big body shriveled and wasting away under the terrific fever that raged within him! Even there, behind locks and bars, the blight of the Blazing Eye had reached him and fulfilled the threat that glowed on his forehead until the consuming flames licked over his parched, shriveled skin....

There was little to be said as Wentworth and Kirkpatrick turned away from the blackened skeleton. This brazenly committed murder, within the very walls of headquarters, had put the police department to scorn. But his own efforts to cope with the Blazing Eye had been equally unsuccessful, Wentworth admitted, as he started back to Sutton Place.

Four members of the Alden-Harmon Expedition had appealed to him for help and had been murdered almost under his eyes. Despite his efforts to combat them, the Oriental killers were becoming even more daring in their merciless scourging of the helpless city. And Nita was in their hands—might already have been horribly slain....

WENTWORTH PACED the living room restlessly, stared out at the dark river and then turned back to where the corpse of Morton Cramer had confronted him—but he was not at home more than five minutes when a caller arrived to see him, a dark-skinned, round-faced man whom Jenkyns announced as Hoong Gow.

Hoong Gow entered the living room confidently but respectfully. He bowed to Wentworth and took the seat proffered him. His birthplace was in the Weikhan Province of Tibet, he answered Wentworth's question. He enjoyed very much living in America. He enjoyed very much meeting Mr. Wentworth. And then….

"I have come to you as an emissary from those who are holding captive your fiancée, Miss Nita van Sloan," he admitted blandly. "I have come with a car which will take you to her."

"That is considerate of you, Hoong Gow," Wentworth answered, as calmly, "but what makes you think that I shall accept your invitation?"

"Because I respect your intelligence, Mr. Wentworth," the Oriental was imperturbable. "I know that you know that Miss van Sloan's safety will depend upon you going with me—that your compliance is, indeed, her only hope of salvation."

The man was about Ram Singh's size and height, Wentworth had noted as soon as he was admitted; his coloring was almost as dark as the Sikh's. From the moment he stepped into the room Wentworth had known what to expect—and had been swiftly planning to cope with the situation. Hoong Gow was a courageous man, no doubt about that; but his courage was partly the fatalism of the East and partly the assurance that Wentworth would not dare to make any attempt against him for fear of reprisals against Nita.

But in that he was wrong.

"There is wisdom in that observation," Wentworth admitted, "but first there are certain details of which we must speak."

For several minutes he engaged the Tibetan in conversation,

but on Wentworth's part that conversation was double-edged. As soon as Jenkyns had admitted the visitor, Wentworth had signaled the butler that he wanted Ram Singh to take his place in a position from which he would be able to hear and see what went on in the living room. Now his words were addressed to the Sikh more than to Hoong Gow; veiled words which Ram Singh would understand.

"There is, as you say, no choice for me but to accompany you, Hoong Gow," he capitulated at last.

Donning his coat and hat, he started out with the Oriental—but when they reached the foyer Hoong Gow suddenly was swept off his feet. Ram Singh's strong arms wrapped around him and held him helpless, while Jackson lifted his legs and helped carry him to a settee. Swiftly they stripped him of his outer garments and bound and gagged him. Then Ram Singh got busy with a pair of scissors and a razor. Off came the beard which he always kept so carefully groomed. With the bound Hoong Gow as a model, Wentworth set to work with his make-up kit—and in a few minutes Ram Singh, in the Tibetan's clothing, was a very creditable duplicate of the fellow.

"Good enough to get by in the dark—unless you have to speak," Wentworth decided, as they started downstairs to the waiting car.

There was a driver at the wheel and a man beside him, Wentworth surveyed swiftly as they approached the sedan. But the back seat was empty. A Chinese driver and a Hindu guard. Would they be suspicious? Would they detect anything wrong? Would they ask questions and force Ram Singh to speak? Wentworth walked forward, tense, his hand ready to flash to his automatic at the first break.

"You first, my dear Hoong Gow," he bowed sardonically at the door, and Ram Singh stepped into the car.

Wentworth followed—and the moment he closed the door the car started forward without a word being exchanged!

So far, they had gotten off with it—but as the sedan sped through the night he soon spotted another car that was following it; and then a second. The odds would be overwhelming....

CHAPTER 7
FACE TO FACE

WENTWORTH WAS riding straight into a death trap, he knew that. Once he stepped across the threshold of the place to which he was being taken, his life would hang in the balance every moment—and yet now his greatest concern was that nothing should occur to prevent him from being admitted there. Tensely he watched the two Orientals in the front seat; felt Ram Singh's arm tauten, his hand steal toward the handle of his long knife, as the man beside the driver turned around.

But the fellow seemed to have no suspicion that everything was not as it should be behind him.

"It is time that his eyes were bound," he directed. "You have the blindfold, Hoong Gow. And see to it that he has no weapons. Search him carefully."

Without replying, Ram Singh fumbled in his coat pockets until his fingers encountered a prepared blindfold. Carefully he tied it around Wentworth's eyes and then ran his hands over his master's body, to lift the twin automatics from their shoulder holsters and slip them into his own pockets. The guard in the front seat had watched his every move, but now, satisfied, he turned back to stare through the windshield.

Ram Singh had had to fasten the blindfold securely in order to escape suspicion, Wentworth realized; but the bandage increased his nervous strain. Now he could no longer watch the Orientals, had to depend entirely upon the Sikh—but a thrill of satisfaction ran through him when one of his guns was surreptitiously pressed into his hand. First one and then, after he had time to holster it, the other.

The comforting feel of the cold steel gave him new confidence, eased his taut nerves so that he could lean back, relaxed, against the seat until the car slackened speed. They were coming to a stop. *Where?*

Ram Singh understood his question. His knee, against Wentworth's, noiselessly coded the answer with imperceptible nudges. They were on Twenty-sixth Street, west of Eighth Avenue—a four-story building.

Then the car came to a halt. The doors opened. Wentworth felt Ram Singh grasp him by the arm, help him out onto the sidewalk. One of the Orientals seemed to be leading the way. There was the sound of an iron gate opening and closing, a few more steps, the echo of the bell inside the building, and then the sound of a door opening. Ram Singh's grip on his arm tightened, and Wentworth stepped inside.

Behind him he heard the door close, heard a key turn in the

lock; and then Ram Singh was leading him down what seemed to be a long passageway, was turning to pass through a doorway that brushed against his arm.

At last the blindfold was taken off—and Wentworth found himself, like a candidate in a lodge initiation, standing in the center of a large, dimly lit, Oriental-caparisoned room. A room that was lined on two sides by a score of Orientals and four white women, who huddled at their feet on the floor. One of those women was Nita! Wentworth caught her eyes upon him, read the stark terror for him that distended them.

"You shouldn't have come, Dick!" she cried miserably. "This is a trap—nothing else! They will burn you!"

But at that moment the wall at the farther end of the room seemed to crack down the middle, and both sides moved silently apart like folding doors. Behind them was a small anteroom that was almost completely occupied by a dais with a throne-like chair in which sat a masked figure attired in elaborate and costly Oriental robes.

The robes of Genghis Khan—and that mask was a counterpart of the features of the Mongol conqueror!

"You are bold, Mr. Wentworth," a hollow-sounding voice taunted him from behind the mask, and Wentworth could see eyes glinting at him from the almond-shaped slits. "You are too bold, that is your misfortune. Otherwise you would have been sufficiently wise to have kept out of my affairs. Instead of that, you have put me to considerable inconvenience by your meddling—but now that is ended."

"I took you at your word," Wentworth flung at him contemptuously. "I came here voluntarily, to insure Miss van Sloan's safety—"

"And I shall live up to my part of that invitation," the hollow, disguised voice mocked at him. "Your presence here does insure

Like a pack of wolves the Orientals closed

in on the two in the center of the floor!

Miss van Sloan's safety. Had you not come, she would have been nothing more than a blackened skeleton in a very short while— but since you are here, yours will be the privilege of taking her place!

"You have been so curious about the working of the Blazing Eye that I am going to give you an opportunity for firsthand experiment, Mr. Wentworth. I want you to know just how it feels to have its stare boring into you—how it feels to burn alive because you were too big a fool to mind your own business!"

Ram Singh and the Hindu who had ridden on the front seat of the sedan had been standing beside Wentworth, holding him between them. Now, at a nod from the masked figure, the Hindu released his grip and stepped back to join his fellows—but Ram Singh stayed where he was.

And then things started to happen with such speed that Wentworth could hardly follow them.

THE DIM lights were fading, and on the wall behind the throne of the Genghis Khan masquerader a faintly outlined, almond-shaped eye began to take form. In a quick side-glance Wentworth caught the gleam of knives in the hands of the Orientals—ready to drive him back into the deadly path of the Blazing Eye should he try to escape from it. At the same instant Nita's voice rang through the room shrilly. She leaped up, made a desperate attempt to rush to him, but strong arms seized her and held her back.

"Run, Dick!" she screamed. "Don't stand there—you will burn!"

Her panic-stricken plea was echoed by Ram Singh's deep rumble.

"We can wait no longer, *sahib*," he said softly. "The hour of death is at hand—but many shall go with us into eternity." His long, hungry knife was unsheathed, eager. "Have I your permission, *sahib?*"

Wentworth's guns leaped into his hands—but it was Ram

Singh who saved him from the ghastly death of the Blazing Eye. Not by the long knife he was so eager to wet—but because he had not fallen back with the other guard; because he stood there and was recognized as an impostor!

"That is not Hoong Gow!" one of the Orientals yelled. "He is an intruder—a faker!"

Pandemonium echoed that warning cry. The masked Genghis Khan sprang to his feet, grasping the arms of his chair.

"Seize him!" he shouted above the din. "Seize him! Take him alive! I do not want him killed!" Like a pack of wolves the Orientals closed in on the two in the center of the floor; but Wentworth breathed a sigh of relief... The lights had brightened again and the devilish mechanism of the Blazing Eye had not gone into operation. With a grim smile on his face he poured bullets into those murderous devils, while Ram Singh's razor-sharp knife seemed to fill the air, to erect a wall of steel at his back and sides.

If he only could get at that masked fiend....

But the Orientals gave him no chance for that. With a savage rush that took no account of the death that flamed from his gun muzzles, they closed in on him and were all over him. Flashing knives arced and stabbed at him, ripped at his coat and grazed his neck, struck sparks from his automatics as he used them to smash the seeking blades out of the way.

Twice he went down under the press of bodies—and came up again with guns blazing. Once he stood over Ram Singh until the Sikh could get back onto his feet, and again he saved his man's life when a treacherous knife thrust would have disemboweled him. But that could not go on—they would be cut down and hacked to pieces by the infuriated Orientals.

Wentworth's breath was coming hard; his arms were tiring from the sheer weight he was holding off and thrusting away from him. Desperately he mustered his strength, put all of it into one mighty lunge, one last effort to break through that savage pack—and he succeeded. For a moment he staggered free—and then reeled back in amazement, hardly believing what his eyes beheld.

Through the doorway poured a stream of thugs—grim-faced, tight-lipped thugs, with Carlo Penozzi in the lead!

In the heat of his own desperate battle he had not heard them break into the building, had not heard the din of their guns as they cleared the hallway. There were fully a dozen of them; a dozen of New York's worst killers, come to grips at last with the foreigners who had slain their fellows and horribly murdered their leader.

The Orientals were swept back by that rush, were cut down on every side, their knives ineffectual against the blasting lead that scythed across the room. In a moment the air was redolent of the fumes of burned powder, the floor slippery with blood, the room ringing with shrieks and groans that were audible even above the thunder of the guns. The place had been turned into a shambles so quickly that Wentworth could hardly realize what had happened. Crouched beside Ram Singh, he held his fire—and then spotted his objective. Genghis Khan!

"With me, warrior!" he clipped—and together they charged

low toward the anteroom where the terrified masquerader was frantically diving behind the shelter of his chair.

He saw them coming—in time to whip out a gun from beneath his robes and trigger a shot at Wentworth, a wild shot that came nowhere near its mark. Wentworth's tight-muscled face twisted into a barely discernible grin of satisfaction as he flung himself forward—but before he could reach the dais the sliding doors glided shut. They clicked right in front of his face—and the place of their meeting was almost invisible.

There was no crevice in which to get a purchase, no hope of prying them open—but there must be some other entrance to that anteroom. Wentworth raced back through the furiously raging battle, out into the corridor that led from the doorway to the big room—but that corridor narrowed and vanished before his startled eyes!

Suddenly the house became a bewildering maze. Nothing seemed stationary; nothing stayed where it should be! The walls of the big room were moving, reshaping; the doorway disappeared; the hallway became part of the room. Unsuspected doors opened on every side to accommodate the fleeing Orientals—but when the thugs tried to follow, nothing but solid, unyielding wall confronted them!

And through the acrid powder fumes came the choking smell of smoke! The building was on fire!

ALL THOUGHT of battle dissipated by the fear of being burned alive, of meeting the horrible fate that had been Nick Penozzi's, the gangsters became utterly panic-stricken. Divided up, each man for himself, they frenziedly sought a way of escape—and were picked off, one by one, by the Oriental knife-men who appeared as if by magic, to disappear again before they could be reached.

The room was a trap, Wentworth realized, as he skirted its four sides, now apparently solid-walled and unbroken by a door. Nita was close beside him, guarded by the vigilant Ram Singh; the other prisoners had disappeared, snatched away by their vanishing captors. Penozzi's thugs were almost wiped out; were sprawled on the floor or creeping on their hands and knees, groaning and trying to staunch the blood that spurted from the ugly knife-thrusts that had disabled them. They would be left there, to roast to death as the flames reached that room-trap and enveloped it. Now the smoke was becoming thicker, the fire coming closer. Wentworth coughed as the fumes stung his lungs—and then he saw a gray trickle seeping into the room through what apparently was a solid wall. A concealed doorway!

Carlo Penozzi saw it, too. He leaped toward it—just as the panel opened and a long knife licked out at him. Penozzi would have been a dead man at that moment but for Wentworth's gun-speed. The twin automatics roared just as the knifepoint

· NITA VAN SLOAN ·

sliced into the gangster's chest; roared and cut down the snarling-faced Chinese knife-wielder.

For an instant the man was revealed, tottering as his knees buckled under him. Then he plunged forward—halfway through the panel opening when Wentworth grasped the side and would not let it close. The way out was open!

Wentworth glanced around him. The last of the gangsters was down. Penozzi, beside the panel opening, was on his knees, clutching at his chest to staunch the blood that was staining his shirt. Bending swiftly, Wentworth lifted him, helped him to his feet and pushed him through the opening as Ram Singh followed with Nita.

Beyond the opening was a corridor that led to a stairway—a stairway that must lead to the upper floors and a way of escape. Wentworth started toward it, but Ram Singh hesitated in the panel opening—and then dived back into the corpse-littered room.

"Ram Singh!" Wentworth shouted after him. "Back to me, warrior—there is no time!"

But at that moment the crazy building seemed to suffer another convulsion. The walls rocked dizzily, new ones appeared out of nowhere—and the panel opening was no more. Ram Singh was trapped—and a leaping tongue of livid flame warned Wentworth that there was no time to try to solve the puzzle of reaching him. In another moment they might all be trapped in the roaring furnace he heard crackling all about them.

With a groan he turned away and headed up the stairs. Now....

That stairway led to the second floor—but, like the one below, it proved to be a death trap from which there was no escape. The third was the same, and the fourth—blind hallways that led to nowhere; that kept the trapped prisoners far from windows or doors that might have been their salvation. On that uppermost floor the smoke was so thick that they could hardly breathe—but again it led them to safety when hope was almost gone.

Wentworth's flashlight, spearing through the darkness, caught a current in the choking fog—a roof exit. He could not reach it himself, but Penozzi could. The gangster was barely able to stand, but the blood had stopped flowing from his wound, matted against the bandage Nita had made of his shirt and tied around him.

Lifted on Wentworth's shoulders, he found the scuttle and battered at the lock with an automatic until it broke. With his last bit of strength he lifted the scuttle and threw it clear before Wentworth lowered him back to the floor and turned to Nita.

"You first," Wentworth ordered. "I'll pass him up to you."

First Nita, then Penozzi—and then, between them, they managed to reach down through the scuttle trap and reach Wentworth's hands; managed to hold firm while he climbed up to them and safety. Barely had he climbed free when the roaring flames came funneling up through the trap. By then, the building beneath them was a roaring blaze—but there were three or four more buildings of the same height beside it. Wentworth led the way to the second and pried open the scuttle.

That building was empty, they discovered as they picked their way downstairs. Empty and boarded up, but the lock of the downstairs door yielded, and they slipped out into the crowd that filled the street. Before anyone could stop them, Wentworth led the way to the corner and commandeered a taxi; told the driver to head for Sutton Place.

What he would do when he reached there he was not certain, but now he had two leads on which to work—two sources of information: Hoong Gow and Carlo Penozzi. Hoong Gow, who should know the identity of that Oriental-garbed masquerader; and Carlo Penozzi, who ought to be able to supply the whereabouts of Ansel Alden....

JACKSON MET them at the gates and helped get Penozzi upstairs, but before Wentworth could start his questioning the telephone rang. They were hardly in the house—and yet the moment he picked up the receiver he knew what voice would come over the wire.

"So you got away, my dear Wentworth," the taunting voice of the Genghis Khan mask mocked him. "You escaped the Blazing Eye and you took Nita van Sloan with you. Bravo! But before you stage a premature celebration, let me assure you that now you have revoked the reprieve I granted her. Now you will both die. If you think this is an idle threat—wait and see!"

Wentworth had seen enough of the Blazing Eye's deviltry to know that his threats never were idle—but Wentworth did not intend to be idle, either. Grimly he turned to his captives—to discover that only one of them would be of use to him. Hoong Gow was unconscious.

"That fellow is a contortionist," Jackson explained ruefully. "He had some capsules in his pocket. How he managed to get them out I don't know, but he did. I caught him just as he was picking up one with his teeth. I got that away from him—but how many he swallowed before that is something else again. He fell asleep right after it and has been like that ever since. Doped himself, from the look of his eyes."

Hoong Gow had effectively sealed his lips for some hours—but Carlo Penozzi could talk. The gangster's jaw set stubbornly and his dark eyes blazed with hate and defiance—but the memory of Ram Singh was very fresh in Wentworth's mind.

Pitilessly he grasped the bandage that covered Penozzi's wound and yanked it away. The blood started to flow.

"And it will go on flowing like that until you decide to talk," Wentworth warned him.

That changed Penozzi's mind. He talked promptly.

To Wentworth's surprise, the gangster flatly denied any connection with Ansel Alden. He did admit having been hired to watch Wentworth's home and to follow and seize him at the first opportunity.

"We followed your car in two of our own," he narrated, "but when we broke into that Twenty-fifth Street joint and saw that the gang was the Chinks that done for Nick—then I lost my head, and we sailed into them."

"Who hired you?" Wentworth pressed inexorably. "If it wasn't Alden, who was it? And I want a straight answer—if you know what is good for you, Penozzi."

For a moment it seemed that the gangster would freeze up. His eyes hardened and his jaws set—but the trickle of blood down his chest seemed to bring him to his senses. He wilted.

"Harmon," he gritted. "Dillon Harmon—and I hope to hell he gives you what I oughta given you—if you start mixin' up with him!"

Dillon Harmon! The mild-mannered scientist was the last person Wentworth would have connected with this program of kidnapping and torture and murder. The idea seemed preposterous—but Wentworth had had experience with other mild-mannered individuals whom nobody had considered capable of the criminal schemes that sprang from their warped brains.

"I am paying Dillon Harmon a visit," he decided quickly. "While I am away you are in charge, Jackson. Look after Miss van Sloan, and keep an eye on our guests—especially Hoong Gow. He may be expecting callers and have decided to have a nap until they come for him."

DILLON HARMON was known as something of a recluse. He lived in the family mansion in fashionable Kew Gardens and seldom left the place—so, at least, was the common belief. But as Wentworth drove one of his powerful-engined coupés across the Queensborough Bridge and along Queens Boulevard he was busily delving into his memory, bringing up little-regarded items that took on new significance in the light of Penozzi's disclosure.

It was Dillon Harmon who had originated the idea of the Alden-Harmon Expedition and secured his father's backing for it. Dillon Harmon had engaged Alden and most of the other members; and Dillon Harmon had helped to lay out the route. So that it would include Sachi-buluk—with the shrine at Kur-ogan close by? Dillon Harmon, through his research work, might well have learned of the existence of that shrine and the ruby-eyed Genghis Khan. And it was not too far-fetched to imagine that the scientist, steeped in the lore of the Orient, had conceived the mad idea of this Genghis Khan cult and wanted the ruby eyes for their mystical significance....

The downstairs windows of the mansion were aglow as Wentworth parked at the curb just beyond it and switched off his lights. It was just one o'clock, he noticed. He had lived through an eternity since the Deacon had taken him into the Chapel of the Eye less than five hours before!

For a while, during those action-packed hours, it had seemed that the master of the Blazing Eye was just about invincible. He had taken every trick. But since then the tide had turned. Wentworth had rescued Nita, had forced the master-murderer to destroy what apparently was his headquarters—and now might be moving in to confront the arch-fiend himself....

There were cars at the rear of the drive that ran along one side of the house, he noticed as he stealthily approached the building. Three cars—all dark. He was almost upon them before he discovered that there was a man watching them—and in that moment he gave fervent thanks for the precaution that had impelled him to keep to the bushes as he neared the building.

The fellow had cupped his hands in front of his face to light a cigarette, and in the match-flame Wentworth caught a glimpse of a hard, knife-scarred countenance. The face of a thug—a gang bruiser!

What was he doing there outside the Harmon home at one o'clock in the morning? One of Dillon Harmon's thugs? Did that mean that there were others inside, taking orders from him at that very moment?

Cautiously Wentworth backed through the shrubbery and approached the house from the other side. On that side was a low, shrubbery-bordered sun porch with French windows behind it Wentworth pounded up onto it, pressed close to one of the panes that was not quite covered by the floor-length drapes—and peered in at a scene that amazed him and brought all his newly-formed theories tumbling down around his ears....

Dillon Harmon was sitting there in the richly furnished living room—but he was perched on the edge of a straight-backed chair, while eight hard-faced gangsters ringed him in and leered at him. Harmon's sweat-beaded face was ashen with terror as one of the thugs grabbed his hand and rubbed his fingers across the glinting blade of a mean-looking knife.

"Nice and sharp, ain't it?" the fellow chuckled. "Ever had a shave with a razor like that? Well, you're gonna get one now. Maybe it'll take most of your hide off—but that's your lookout. Start talking—unless you want me to begin."

"I can't—I don't know anything about it," Dillon Harmon quavered. "I tell you I know nothing about any rubies, Alden!" he turned beseechingly to a far corner of the room—where Wentworth, following his frantic gaze, spied Ansel Alden standing with Hy Markin, one of the well-known Penozzi lieutenants!

Ansel Alden! So the explorer was the man behind the Penozzi mob! Carlo Penozzi had known that Markin and this delegation of cutthroats would be there at the Harmon home with him; had deliberately sent Wentworth into what he was sure would prove to be a death trap!

But Carlo Penozzi had misfigured once that night, and now his calculations were going to miscarry a second time.

Wentworth backed away from the window and knelt beside the low stone railing that surrounded the porch. Out of his pocket came his make-up kit. Carefully he propped up the mirror so that he could take advantage of what light came from inside—and then he went to work. Swiftly and surely his expert fingers completed the transformation, and when the black cape and floppy-brimmed hat came from inside the lining of his coat it was the fearsome, incredibly ugly Spider, a skulking, shadowy creature of the night, who drew back from the French windows and crouched low for a charge.

"Suppose we start here," the thug who towered over Dillon Harmon jeered—and the knife grazed the side of the scientist's head, to cut into the skin as if it would shear off an ear.

Harmon moaned as blood started running down his cheek—but suddenly the sound was lost in another that blotted it out. With a wild, maniacal yell, calculated to terrify any who heard it, the Spider hurled himself forward. His down-smashing automatic and his left shoulder hit one of the long panes together and shattered the glass into a thousand splinters. Through the window he hurtled, his guns blazing even before his feet touched the floor.

Two of those thugs died before they could turn their heads. The torturer followed them before he could whirl to fling his knife at the terrifying specter that suddenly confronted them. Like an unholy hobgoblin that had suddenly burst from the nether regions, the Spider charged across that room and was in the midst of them, pounding his guns into their faces, blasting a hail of lead into them before they could reach their weapons. Death had overwhelmed them, stretched half their number on the floor and sent the others fleeing wildly for their lives, But it was not these small fry whom Wentworth wanted. Straight across the room toward Ansel Alden he headed.

Alden saw him coming. The flinty eyes were cold as ice in the bleak, bulldog face. He tensed, but he seemed to make no attempt to draw a weapon; no attempt to defend himself until

Wentworth was almost upon him. But then he moved swiftly—every inch the steel-nerved adventurer who boasted that he could meet any situation that confronted him.

Instead of taking flight like the others, he suddenly rushed forward and grabbed hold of Hy Markin; lifted the little gangster bodily—and hurled him straight at the Spider! Hy Markin died with Wentworth's lead in his brain, but the impact of his body swept Wentworth off his feet; and by the time he had picked himself up from the hard floor Ansel Alden was gone....

Throughout that fusillade of shots Dillon Harmon had sat on the edge of his chair like a statue, his eyes great pools of fright. Now he tried to speak, but his tongue clove to the roof of his mouth. Fascinated, he watched that grotesque, black-caped figure hover over the bodies of the dead gangsters like a great vulture—watched something shiny in his hand press down on the dead foreheads and leave there the crimson imprint of a spider. He stirred.

"Thanks—Spider," he managed to summon his voice and make his trembling lips move.

But the ebon-clad figure was peering at a Tibetan prayer wheel that stood, half-concealed, on a shelf in a shadowy corner of the room; was taking it down and examining it carefully.

"Morton Cramer brought that back from Asia," Harmon ventured timidly. "If you would like to have me give it to you—"

"No," the Spider's voice croaked. "I just want—*this.*"

As he spoke he took the wheel apart, pried open the hub with a pocketknife—and spilled out a blood-red gem the size of a large pecan, the gleaming eye of Genghis Khan!

In the palm of his hand Wentworth held the stone for which Alden and the Penozzis had been hunting, the stone Cramer had tried so desperately to defend, the stone because of which men had died in agony—and as he studied it closely he suspected what, in the morning, he was to find was true: it was nothing more than an almost worthless carnelian....

CHAPTER 8
MEN OF THE HILLS

CARLO PENOZZI stared as if he were face to face with a ghost when Wentworth stepped into the Sutton Place living room and confronted him. His cheeks blanched and his eyes were wide and fear-shot as he got to his feet—and then dropped back resignedly onto the couch where he had been dozing under Jackson's watchful eyes.

"Jeez—you must have more lives than a cat!" he tacitly admitted the trap that had failed.

"And so has your friend Ansel Alden," Wentworth snapped.

Penozzi's eyes narrowed, became hard.

"So he got clear, too," he spat in disgust. "I didn't expect you'd get out of that alive—I admit it, Wentworth. I don't like you; your kind and mine don't mix—and I ain't at all sure that you didn't have a hand in burning Nick. But I was hoping to hell you'd finish Alden before you got yours. We've had nothing but trouble since he got hold of Nick—and I never trusted him from the start. Guess they didn't get the rocks then?" He eyed Wentworth cagily. "If they did, Markin would've taken care of him—"

Then he seemed to realize that he was saying too much. His jaws snapped shut and he lapsed into sullen silence.

Wentworth regarded him thoughtfully. So that set-up at the Harmon home had been a double trap—for both Ansel Alden and himself. And, had the gems for which they searched been found, the thugs no doubt would have rounded out the job by murdering Dillon Harmon as well. Alden might be well able to handle himself in the wilds, but when he started mixing with New York gangsters he had gotten into deeper water than he suspected.

But there was nothing more to be gained by keeping Carlo Penozzi a prisoner. Now that his connection with Ansel Alden was established, there seemed to be nothing more that the gangster could divulge. On the other hand, free, he might prove to be very useful; might serve as the means of locating Ansel Alden....

"I don't know what you expect, Penozzi," Wentworth eyed the sullen gang leader. "Probably a trip to the bottom of the river with a load of scrap iron tied around your neck. That is what you deserve—and what you no doubt would give me; but I am going to turn you loose.

"Jenkyns," he turned to his old butler, "go down and see if you can get him a cab."

Jenkyns got the cab, and a few minutes later they helped Penozzi into it; watched it head toward Sutton Place and disappear around the corner.

"You arranged it?" Wentworth turned back to the building.

"Easily, sir," Jenkyns assured. "That was one of the regular drivers from the line on the next corner. I gave him five dollars.

He will be back with the address as soon as he disposes of his fare."

Wentworth nodded. So much for Penozzi. Now there remained only Hoong Gow. The Tibetan still slept soundly, undisturbed by shaking and face-slapping. The drug he had taken must have been a powerful one—but his own people would have known how to rouse him from its stupor. Hot irons under the feet or sharp splinters of bamboo driven under the fingernails were remarkably effective restoratives—but for a white man such practical measures were tabu.

Wentworth sighed—with what was almost regret. Sometimes white civilization imposed handicaps that hardly seemed fair; handicaps of which these calculating Orientals were very ready to take advantage. He could not torture Hoong Gow—and yet behind those sleep-sealed lips might lie the answer that would save hundreds, perhaps thousands, of innocent New Yorkers from a horrible death....

Standing over the inert form, Wentworth was still debating how to bring the man back to consciousness when the telephone rang. Abstractedly he lifted the receiver—and then tensed as if he listened to a voice that came straight from the grave!

"Forgive me if I have caused you uneasiness, master," Ram Singh's deep, nasal voice rang in his ear, "but this is the first opportunity I have had to reach a telephone—"

"Ram Singh!" Wentworth boomed. "Where are you, man?"

"At present, in the telephone booth of a drugstore, but I must return quickly to a building on West Forty-eighth Street," the Sikh answered and furnished the complete address. "It is above

119

It was a ghastly, barbarous spectacle and it held every man in the room terrified!

121

a Hindu restaurant; the rear room on the second floor. If you will come quickly, *sahib*, it may be that we can accomplish much in a short time."

Ram Singh—alive! Wentworth had had little time to mourn the faithful Sikh in the past few hours, but he had felt his loss keenly.

WENTWORTH WAITED only to insist that Nita retire. Then he hastened to the West Side address and was met by Ram Singh at the door; was admitted to a large bedroom that was equipped with teakwood furnishings and hung with Indian rugs and draperies. On a rug-covered couch lay a man whom Wentworth recognized with an amazed start. The Hindu guard who had ridden beside the driver in the sedan that took him to the headquarters of the master of the Blazing Eye!

Ram Singh read his thoughts and answered before he could put them into words.

"This unworthy one is no Hindu, *sahib*," he apologized. "Shame is mine to admit it, but he is of my own people, a Sikh. I recognized that as soon as I sighted his face in the car—but my shame would not let me mention it. In the hills we have a saying that a man is like a rock torn loose from the hillside; the greater the height from which it falls, the deeper it digs into the mud. Such a one is this Gura Singh—a Sikh who had forgotten the one true God and had turned to the worship of a man who is dead these hundreds of years!"

"But how did you get here?" Wentworth could not restrain his question. "I tried to stop you, but when the walls of that doomed building closed around you I thought that you were lost."

"He is a Sikh, and when I turned to look back into that room I saw that he still lived; I had to go back, *sahib,*" Ram Singh said simply. "He knew a way out, and I was able to carry him there just in time to escape the flames. For that, by our hill law, his life is mine to do with as I wish. For that, he will obey me—and you, *sahib,* and will attempt to atone for the harm he has done."

"*Wah, sahib,* that I will—gladly," Gura Singh bowed his head humbly.

"He has been a follower of this man whom you seek, master," Ram Singh silenced him. "He knows much of the evil doings—"

"The identity of this man—does he know that?" Wentworth interrupted eagerly, but Ram Singh shook his head regretfully.

"Not that, master. Very few, it seems, know that. But tomorrow is to be a day of importance; a day for which men are being brought here from other cities. This Gura Singh waits to enlist two other Sikhs who have fallen as low as he. They will be here shortly, *sahib;* in the early hours of the morning. We shall receive them when they arrive—and shall take their places tomorrow."

Ram Singh had made all the preparations. The make-up he had worn to pass as Hoong Gow was removed and a turban was once more bound around his head, the mate to another which he had in readiness for Wentworth. A coat of brown stain on his face and neck and hands, a few minutes of work with his make-up kit, black dye in his hair, and Wentworth was a thoroughly convincing Sikh, ready to take the place of one of the Blazing Eye's new recruits.

Shortly after five o'clock the new men arrived. Gura Singh answered their ring and ushered them into the room—where the cold muzzles of automatics pressed close against the backs of their necks quickly subjugated them. While they stood helpless, Gura Singh tied them up securely and made them comfortable on lounges where they would spend the rest of the day.

"It is unlikely that you will need credentials, *sahib*, but it might be well to take these should they be necessary," he suggested, as he passed over the papers he took from the bound men's pockets. "You, *sahib*, will be Rangoor Singh, and Ram Singh will take the place of Booja Singh."

Carefully they rehearsed their roles, so that by the time they left with Gura Singh for a noonday meeting they had their stories letter-perfect. The rendezvous was in the restaurant on the floor below, but a car soon arrived to take them to the real gathering place.

A Chinese restaurant not more than three blocks away, that proved to be. Wentworth made note of the number, glanced up and down the block so as to be able to describe it perfectly if he could reach a telephone. Then he was inside, following Gura Singh into a back room—and through the door of a closet into the building next door!

That building was a closed-up hotel. From the outside it appeared to be long-abandoned, the windows and doors boarded up and bill-posted, an accumulation of wind-blown rubbish on the steps—but inside the scene was far different What had been the dining room was transformed into the counterpart of an Oriental temple. Rugs and drapes covered the walls, flickering lamps that lit the place dimly hung from the ceiling, and at one end stood an elaborate altar with steps leading to its top—an altar with a life-sized picture of Genghis Khan set in a strange shadow-frame directly behind it.

Rangoor Singh and Booja Singh had little difficulty passing inspection. They were accepted without question when Gura Singh vouched for them. Unnoticed among the others, they found places in the semicircle of thirty or more Orientals who squatted on the floor and waited for the service to begin. Keenly Wentworth studied them, recognized men of ten or more tribes and nationalities, until the dull boom of a temple gong brought them all to attention.

"Now," Gura Singh whispered, as he went to his knees to form part of the semicircle that faced the altar.

INSTANTLY THE buzz of conversation was hushed. Expectant faces turned toward the altar, dark eyes stared as if to witness the performance of a miracle, and one by one the lamps were snuffed out—until only the altar was illuminated; only the picture of Genghis Khan behind it. Weirdly the light from hidden bulbs played upon it, until there seemed to be nothing in that big room but the picture—nothing but that lifelike figure that almost breathed—that *did* breathe! One moment that portrayal of Genghis Khan was no more than a flat oil painting; in the next it was indefinably modeled, as if the painting itself was coming to life—and then it was alive; was walking down the steps from the altar, to stand there in front of it. The same Oriental-gowned figure he had seen on Twenty-fifth Street, Wentworth identified the masquerader—but when he glanced around at his neighbors he saw that these men actually believed that they had witnessed a transfiguration. They actually believed that they had witnessed the reincarnation of Genghis Khan right there in their midst!

"The day of our new empire marches on," the hollow, sonorous voice boomed out from behind the mask. "The moment of our victory is close at hand. First this city, then this country, then this continent—and after that the Holy Empire of Genghis Khan will stretch from pole to pole and will girdle the earth! The empire of the brown and yellow men, when white domination will be a thing of the past!"

They answered him with murmurs and sighs, with the rapt lip-working of spellbound devotees listening to a pronunciamento from their god—and as Wentworth watched that weird performance cold fear gripped him. These men were no longer sane but tools in the hands of this cunning schemer—worse than an army of savages turned loose on the city!

"Today we strike a blow that will leave this city cowering," the hollow voice boomed again; and now Wentworth noticed something peculiar about its timbre—something almost hypnotic that began to grip him despite himself. "Tomorrow we follow that with a stroke that will bring New York to its knees. Before the end of this week we will be undisputed masters here and be ready to extend our conquest—but first we must be sure of ourselves. First we must be certain that there are no weaklings and no traitors!"

The eyes behind the mask swept the semicircle; seemed to bore into each face, eerily illumined by the reflected light from behind the altar. That gaze settled on him, and Wentworth tensed, certain that he was about to be unmasked. His fingers stretched out, ready to flash to his holster—but in that moment he caught the flash of light on metal that came from the drapes no more than ten feet from him, and he knew that he would have no chance to make a draw. Eagle-eyed killers were stationed all around that room, watching every moment, ready to shoot down the first man who made a suspicious move.

But the searching gaze traveled on over the semicircle, and then the booming voice resumed.

"There are those who have failed, those who have tried to betray us, those who would not be warned—and for them there is only one reward," he announced. "For them there is only the cold embrace of death!"

As he spoke he clapped his hands, and the heavy drapes at one side of the room parted, to reveal an alcove in which another Genghis Khan sat on a platform! For a moment the figure was indistinct, but as the lights in the alcove brightened Wentworth saw that this figure was made of metal—a metal Genghis Khan upon a metal throne.

And seated on the floor beneath that throne were half a dozen prisoners, their mouths gagged, their arms and legs tightly bound.

Two of them were Chinese. Two more he recognized as members of the Penozzi gang. Another seemed to be a prosperous looking businessman, while the sixth had all the earmarks of one of Stanley Kirkpatrick's detectives. Six men who knew they were doomed and stared out at the assemblage with frightened eyes set in tense, perspiration-bathed faces.

"Death is their due," the masked figure boomed again, "but there is not time now to dispose of them all. For the present, only one shall die—the one fate shall choose."

Out from behind the metal image one of the attendants pushed a small wheeled table with a prayer wheel in its center. Slowly the masquerader turned the wheel and scrutinized it, seemed to read each of the prayers attached to the paddle wheels—and then he spun it sharply and stepped back to watch it with gloating eyes.

"Fate will decide," he repeated. "Fate will decide the one on whom the Eye will fix!"

The Eye! Only then did Wentworth notice that there was a rod behind the prayer wheel, a rod with an almond-shaped eye at its top. Suddenly the eye lit up and seemed to stare down at the wheel whirling just below it—and in that moment Wentworth understood the fiendish cruelty of the terrible game he was watching; understood why the bound victims craned their necks and stared up at the revolving wheel with such horrible fascination.

For them, that was the wheel of life and death, the Blazing Eye their merciless executioner looking down not at fluttering prayer slips but at slips of paper which bore their names!

Now the wheel was slowing its pace. Slowing more and more, until it was hardly moving. And then it stopped entirely; stopped with that miniature Blazing Eye staring down at a slip of paper attached to a paddle wheel that was just beneath it.

With maddening deliberation the masked figure lifted the slip and bent over to read it

"Angelo Ruvelo!" he boomed out the name—and one of those bound victims struggled so frantically that he got to his knees and then rolled over on his face, to thresh madly on the floor as two powerful Orientals approached and lifted him easily.

RUVELO WAS one of Penozzi's meanest killers, a man who stood convicted in the underworld of crimes that no self-respecting gunman would have considered; but in that moment Richard Wentworth pitied him. Apoplectic with terror, he could do nothing to help himself or ward off a fate which he must have seen meted out to others.

On the lap of the metal Genghis Khan they placed him; held him there until the image began to move. The arms came up from the arms of the chair and wrapped so tightly around the writhing victim that he could no longer move. For long moments he was held there, while every eye in that big room was riveted upon him—and then, suddenly, his doom was upon him.

That insensate image became a thing of fire! From dozens of unseen jets flames poured, bathing the metal statue from top to bottom in rippling waves of fire. In a moment Ruvelo's clothing kindled and burned to ashes, to drop from the singed flesh as he writhed in fearful paroxysms.

A ghastly, barbarous spectacle—but it held every man in that room, fascinated and terrified. Each could see his own body being consumed by those terrible flames—the reward of disobedience or failure! This diabolical Genghis Khan was missing no bet; was binding these fanatical followers to him with the even stronger chains of mortal terror....

Tensely Wentworth watched that shocking cremation; held himself rigidly in check while Ruvelo's body was burned to ashes. His every impulse was to fling himself upon that masked fiend, to put a bullet through the monster's head and end his devilment for all time—but that, he knew, he could not hope to accomplish.

There was nothing to do but squat there on his knees, with the gagging stench of roasting flesh in his nostrils, the hiss of sizzling blood in his ears, until what had been Angelo Ruvelo was nothing more than ashes and blackened, glowing bones that dropped out of the metal arms. Not until then did Genghis Khan turn away from the sickening sight and face his fascinated followers.

"This afternoon," his voice started low and increased in volume as it stole into their mesmerized brains and took complete possession of them, "we strike with the speed of lightning and teach this city that nowhere is there safety unless Genghis Khan so decrees it. This afternoon we turn New York's largest department store into a mammoth morgue!

"The plans have all been completed," his words increased in tempo, snapped at them like bullets from a machine-gun. "Your leaders all know their duties and will assign each of you to his part. There will be no danger; every contingency has been covered. At three o'clock this afternoon Macy's department store will be crowded with customers shopping for their Easter finery.

At three-fifteen it will be filled with writhing bodies—an object lesson that this city will never forget!"

Macy's! Wentworth was stunned by the enormity of the horror he visualized! Little more than a week before Easter, the store would be jammed with thousands of shoppers, crowded from counter to counter with helpless women. To turn the Blazing Eye loose on them would be appalling!

Somehow, he must get out of there—must get in touch with Stanley Kirkpatrick; but he soon discovered that escape was practically impossible. It had been easy to get into that place, but now alert guards were stationed at the doors, and keen, probing eyes watched every move. Wentworth had to be careful, desperately careful, not to betray his anxiety, for now he was certain of those hidden marksmen who kept the entire room constantly under cover. He was in a trap from which there was no escape.

"You have not been assigned, have you, Sikh?" a button-eyed Japanese stepped in front of him and looked him over. "You will do for my detail—without that turban. Take it off. We are to be in charge of the Broadway doors."

The doors—that might afford an opportunity to escape!

Wentworth's hopes fell when he saw that Ram Singh was enlisted for a party which was to handle the upper floors of the building. Not satisfied with making a ghastly shambles of the main floor, this ruthless devil intended to spread death throughout the entire huge store!

Perhaps there would be a way of escape—even though it meant condemning Ram Singh to death with the others. That was a sacrifice that would have to be made to save thousands of lives....

WENTWORTH CLUNG to that hope—but when he arrived at the store with his companions he soon discovered that it was vain. He was watched constantly; was shepherded so carefully by the Japanese that he knew the man was suspicious of him—knew that swift death would be his lot at the merest indication of a hostile move.

Unobtrusively the Orientals filtered into the thronged store. By ones and twos they mingled with the crowd and made their way to their stations. From his position near the Broadway doors Wentworth looked over the shopper-packed main floor—and shuddered at thought of the doom that hung over those unsuspecting women. High above the counters, suspended from the ceiling near the center of the store, was a huge white rabbit, a symbol of the Easter season. Wentworth saw the children looking up at it, pointing to it—and a pang shot through him. Resolutely he took a step toward the door, determined to get out of that trap at any cost—but two of the Orientals were close at his side, blocking his way; and he felt cold steel jammed against his body.

"Not so fast, Sikh," the Japanese gibed at him. "You are too eager; it is still one minute of three."

Sixty seconds more—and then a shrill whistle cut through the buzzing hum of the busy store! A shrill whistle—and the lights went out; all but the dim emergency lights that illumined the crowded aisles weirdly. And then two great, baleful eyes that sprang to life in the head of the huge rabbit—the deadly orbs of the Blazing Eye!

"Quick—the doors!" the Japanese commanded, and his men sprang to press down the floor-bolts that made them fast, then lined up in front of them with quickly drawn guns.

But Wentworth waited no longer. The moment he glimpsed the eyes of that rabbit, he leaped to one side and knocked the Japanese sprawling; sprang past him, straight into the surprised, uncertain crowd. Too late now to attempt to escape; too late to get to a telephone. There was only one hope of saving these people; he must put that rabbit out of commission, must destroy it.

How? It was much too high for him to reach—but as he ran toward it a quick plan took shape in his seething mind. The escalator to the second floor; it might enable him to reach the deadly contraption. But he must do more than that. He must destroy it and at the same time must stampede these murdering devils—must put a fear into them that would be even greater than the terror Genghis Khan held over them.

Even before he reached the escalator, the big rabbit began to turn, its blazing eyes sweeping the store—and as it did a shrill pandemonium broke loose in the jammed aisles. Screams and shrieks, terrified women clawing at one another in a mad stampede to escape from they knew not what. The ghastly mass slaughter had started!

Frantically Wentworth raced up the escalator steps, thrusting surprised women out of his way, until he reached the second floor. Behind a counter he flung himself, to go to work with his make-up kit faster than he had ever worked in his life. There was no time to attempt to remove the brown stain. That must remain. The Spider's make-up went on top of it; and when the black cape and hat were in place, it was a hideous, brown-faced Spider who leaped from behind the counter and ran to the far end of the escalator well.

In his hands he clutched a long silken rope, a strand of the Spider's web, that he had unwound from around his waist, beneath his vest. Swiftly he fastened it to a pillar and dropped it down over the lower end of the escalator, to slide down its length and swing there until he could reach the side of the companion escalator shaft with his feet—then to thrust himself far out into the air. Like a pendulum he swung there, wider and wider in his arc—until he let go in mid-air and sailed straight at the blazing-eyed rabbit.

His arms closed around it, barely missed one of the luminous eyes. Quickly he climbed up on it, his automatic in his hand, blasting away at the wire cables that held it, severing them. But now the Orientals realized what he was doing. Bullets drove at him, whipped through his black cape, riddled the rabbit. At any moment they must bring him down—but before that happened the cables were blasted away, and the big papier-maché contraption crashed to the floor and smashed to bits.

The magnet was destroyed, and now, Wentworth was almost certain, the fiendish death-machines would not work!

He was right. Again the shrill whistle cut through the awful bedlam that raged in the stricken store. Out from behind the counters where they had been hiding leaped the Orientals who had been operating the death broadcasters. Desperately he attempted to reach them, to shoot them down—but the terrified crowd got in his way, hindered him and then tripped him.

The Orientals made good use of that opportunity to escape with their devilish mechanisms—but there still were some on the upper floors. Howling like a madman, Wentworth fought his way up one of the jammed escalators, scaring the terrified shoppers out of his way.

They were fleeing to the main floor—but not fleeing from the death of the Blazing Eye. They were being shepherded to it by the Orientals who had been assigned to the upper floors; were being herded downstairs to be slaughtered by the hundreds, piled up in windrows of corpses.

The Spider had already blasted that fiendish scheme, and now his deadly automatics played havoc with the gun-wielding Orientals. When he reached the fourth floor he found Ram Singh already in command there. Together they ranged through the rest of the building, cutting down unmercifully every Oriental who crossed their path.

The master of the Blazing Eye had failed! His fiendish plan had been ruined, and he had lost nearly a score of his killers! WENTWORTH THRILLED with grim satisfaction— and almost forgot his own danger. By the time he and Ram Singh reached the main floor in a commandeered elevator, the store was thronged with policemen. Just in time he slammed the door and ran the elevator to the basement and then to the sub-cellar—from where they were able to dash to the stairs that led up to the Thirty-fifth Street shipping platforms.

A dozen delivery trucks, abandoned by their drivers, who had run into the store, stood at the platforms. Ram Singh leaped into one, sprang to the wheel as Wentworth scrambled in behind him. Out into the street it sped while Wentworth, in the protection of the package compartment, stripped off the Spider's make-up.

As soon as the last vestiges of it were gone, they abandoned the truck and he hurried to a telephone to contact Kirkpatrick.

"I have located the headquarters of the Blazing Eye, Kirk," he snapped the moment the commissioner answered. "Ram Singh and I were in it and have just managed to reach a phone."

Quickly he described the place and agreed to hurry there to await the arrival of Kirkpatrick and his men. That did not take long. The commissioner raced uptown with a screaming motorcycle escort clearing the way. With Wentworth in the lead, they entered the Chinese restaurant and headed for the closet entrance to the hotel—but the closet had disappeared, and the wall seemed to be intact!

"It was right there, that's certain," Wentworth puzzled, as he knelt on the floor and pulled back the linoleum—to reveal a hardly-discernible crack in the floor. "That wall is a fake!" he discovered, as he leaped to his feet. "It has been moved in here in front of the entrance!"

Kirkpatrick was prepared for that. Fire apparatus had come with the police reserves. The firemen went at the wall with their axes, punctured it and tore it to pieces—to reveal a second wall and a doorway beyond it. Through the aperture Kirkpatrick plunged, with Wentworth close at his heels—but just in time Wentworth made a grab for him and flung him back to safety!

The moment their feet had crossed the threshold they had sprung a deadly trap. A tremendous roar shook the building, and the wall came tumbling down on the spot from which they had just leaped. A terrific explosion—and then the fire that leaped out in a dozen places in the abandoned hotel.

Peering through the clouds of thick dust, they could see flames licking the drape-covered walls of the big room, turning it into a huge bonfire. And then, as the drapes which shrouded the torture alcove went up in flames, they saw something else— something that gripped them and held them horrified.

The metal image of Genghis Khan was in operation; was sheathed in flames that roasted the blackened but still writhing form—of Gura Singh!

The Sikh was paying fearfully for his betrayal of Genghis Khan....

For a long moment they stood there spellbound, rooted to the floor—until Ram Singh leaped past them, straight into that inferno. For an instant there was the flash of a long-bladed knife—and then the tortured body was still, Gura Singh's agony ended.

When Ram Singh staggered back to the shattered wall only Wentworth was there to catch him. Stanley Kirkpatrick had turned away, ostensibly to make way for the firemen....

CHAPTER 9
WELCOME—TO DEATH

THE HOLLOW voice of that masquerading Genghis Khan seemed to ring mockingly in Richard Wentworth's ears as he turned away from the smoldering ruins of the empty hotel. The police and firemen had risked their lives daringly to search the doomed, crumbling building, but they had found no trace of the other prisoners. The fiendish master of the Blazing Eye had removed them—had left Gura Singh behind as a brazen defiance; a reminder that he was far from defeated.

Despite the fact that Wentworth had saved thousands of lives, hundreds of women had perished in that demoniacal death trap at Macy's—and that, he remembered, was only to be the preliminary blow, the blow that would stun New York. After it, on the next day, was to come the blow that would bring the city to its knees and horrify the whole nation!

Desperately Wentworth cast about for a way of stopping him; of learning the nature of the intended atrocity. Somewhere there must be a lead to this cunning scoundrel; someone who knew his identity, who could be forced to unveil him. But who?

Hoong Gow? The Tibetan still seemed to be in a coma. He was awake now, but he appeared to be half-doped. Whether or not he was shamming, Wentworth realized that there was no way, short of inhuman torture, of forcing information from his lips. Carlo Penozzi? He was anxious to locate the master of the Blazing Eye on his own account; and so was Ansel Alden.

One after the other, he thought of every possible contact

and dismissed each as hopeless—until the face of Deacon Baumgarten flashed into his mind. The Deacon—he seemed to be well-versed in the inner workings of the Blazing Eye organization! He had known of the intended destruction of Henry Mung's restaurants, and he would know what was planned for the morrow!

Wentworth lost no time seeking him out. An hour later, the frowsy, unkempt figure of Blinky McQuade shuffled out of Holy Alley and made his way toward the coffee pot where the Deacon was most likely to be found. Again he detected that air of suppressed excitement and fear—on passing faces, in quick-flashing eyes that scrutinized him suspiciously.

His own spectacle-masked eyes missed nothing. As he neared the coffee pot he picked out a thug whom he recognized as one of the Penozzi gang lounging beside a pushcart a few yards from the doorway—and then another farther down the street. They had the place bracketed—and Carlo Penozzi was across the way, talking to a third hoodlum in the doorway of the opposite building.

Curiously Wentworth glanced over the occupants of the restaurant as he stepped inside. Three or four youths who were nothing but youngsters, a frowsy bum who was half-asleep at the counter—and the Deacon in his usual place at the rear of the store. He was the only one worth watching—but why had Penozzi put him under surveillance? Did he, too, hope to use the Deacon as a means of reaching the master of the Blazing Eye?

Baumgarten looked up before Blinky reached his table, and

when he glimpsed his visitor the long, lugubrious face twisted into a knowing smile.

"I come back for that free meal you were gonna stake me to, Deacon," Blinky growled as he slumped into a seat across the table and nodded to the counterman. "I ain't forgot about it— just because you give me the slip."

"Ah, yes—we didn't have our snack last evening, did we?" Baumgarten smiled unctuously. "Now I fear we shan't ever be able to have it in the place to which I was taking you. They seem to have had an—accident there last evening. It was fortunate we did not arrive sooner."

"Yeah, it was fortunate—in the pig's neck," Blinky glowered, as he downed his drink and nodded to the counterman for a follow-up. "You didn't happen to amble along there by no accident; don't give me any more of that. I dunno what this is all about, but I want in on it, see? I feel myself getting religion— like you said I oughta."

Quite unperturbed, the Deacon drained his cup and smacked his lips.

"You have seen the light at a good time, Blinky," he endorsed without the trace of a smile. "I think perhaps your particular talents may prove very useful—if you will be free tomorrow?"

Blinky's answer was a snort.

"Excellent," Baumgarten interpreted and then glanced at his watch. "In about ten minutes," he eyed his empty cup significantly, "it will be a good time to take you to the one who handles all such matters."

PENOZZI WAS not in sight, but his hoodlums were still

140

posted outside the coffee pot when Blinky and the Deacon came out; but Baumgarten merely shrugged when Wentworth nudged him. He made no effort to elude them as they shadowed him none too skillfully—until he turned in at the doorway of a tenement just off the end of First Avenue. Down into the cellar he led the way. There he unlocked a rusty iron door that opened into the cellar of the next building, went through that to the back yard and into the cellar door of the loft building that backed up to it from the street beyond.

On the second floor of that building Blinky met "the man who handles such matters"—who proved to be Stud Pokashefsky, a thickset, heavy-jowled politician who was a power in the underworld. "Stud Poker" was holding court in an empty loft that had been converted into a semi-office, semi-clubroom by the addition of a battered desk and several dozen folding chairs. On the latter lounged a score or more men, most of whom were known to Blinky McQuade.

"Safes are your line, eh, McQuade?" Stud Poker peered at him with small, porcine eyes, as he chewed the end of a half-smoked cigar. "Well, we may be able to use you. Don't expect there'll be much crib-cracking to do, though—we expect them to be all open and waiting for us. We're gonna jump in so fast they won't have time to close the doors."

"I don't *hafta* crack cribs," Blinky reminded.

"That's right," Stud grinned. "Guess maybe you *could* work if the doors were open, eh?" he chuckled. "I'll put you down for the crew that'll handle Maiden Lane—might be some of those jewelers' cribs that'll need your special attention. That's eleven tomorrow morning—and no later, remember that. Sam Yarwitz, over there, will give you the rest of the dope."

Yarwitz was busy giving instructions to several others, and, as Blinky listened, the amazing scope of the raid they were planning astounded him. Maiden Lane—that was bad enough. Well below the police deadline, the Lane was supposed to be closed territory to crooks. But Maiden Lane was only one of the streets that had been carefully tabulated and covered. Wall Street, Pine, Liberty, Cedar, Rector, Exchange Place—for all the streets leading from Lower Broadway there were crews; crews for every block of Broadway itself.

"Jim Hoffman will be your crew leader, McQuade," Yarwitz told him. "Know him, don't you? You meet him at eleven o'clock at Maiden Lane and Pearl Street—understand?"

"Yeah, I understand," Wentworth grumbled, "and I understand what'll happen to me if a dick spots me down there, too!"

"Don't worry about that," Yarwitz grinned. "No dick is going to bother you tomorrow morning—no cop either. They'll all be too busy looking the other way, see? We'll go to work a little after twelve. Can't say just how quick—that depends on how long it takes 'em to get up from the Battery; but nobody'll have to tell you when to get started. There'll be plenty of hell let loose. This is going to be a reception the city'll remember for many a day!" he chuckled. "The party they threw for Lindy won't be in it with the one we'll put on!"

A reception! In the stress of the past few days Wentworth had paid little attention to anything but the depredations of the Blazing Eye. But suddenly he understood what Yarwitz meant; realized why this wholesale robbery was to be staged at noon the next day. That was the hour set for the reception to Ben Waldo, the first solo round-the-world flyer who had just landed in New York! The triumphal procession was scheduled to leave the Battery at noon, to pass up Broadway to the City Hall—and while it was making its way through a man-made snowstorm of paper and ticker-tape, this army of thieves was to be let loose on the banks and offices of the lower city, secure in the knowledge that the police would be too busy handling the jubilant crowd to interfere with them!

A daring daylight onslaught that would loot the financial district and leave the city gasping!

Wentworth visualized the fearful panic that would result when the killers turned their guns on the late-arriving police. There would be dozens of innocent bystanders shot down, hundreds trampled underfoot!

An appalling prospect—but suddenly it was dwarfed by the magnitude of a ghastly possibility that swept in upon him. This audacious raid on the city's financial center was the scheme of the Blazing Eye—and that meant that cold-blooded murder, wholesale slaughter, would run hand in hand with the looting! A slaughter that would appall the entire nation!

Grimly he took hold of himself, careful not to give any indication of the rage that seethed within him. The most important thing now was to get out of that place, to get in touch with Kirkpatrick so that the police would be ready to cope with this army of criminals, ready to meet them with blasting guns and smash the terror of this Blazing Eye not only now but for all time....

But just as he was about to leave, footsteps sounded on the stairway—and into the lighted end of the loft stepped a figure who changed that tense situation startlingly!

WHEN STANLEY KIRKPATRICK turned away from the fire-gutted ruins of the hotel that had been a meeting-place for the followers of Genghis Khan, one more hope had gone up into smoke with the burned building. One more hope—and now he knew that he had very few left to lose.

Kirkpatrick was a badly worried man as he started back to headquarters; a tired man who almost felt that the struggle was too much for him. For years he had met criminal onslaughts of every kind, had grimly accepted challenge after challenge and fought doggedly until the law and order which he represented had triumphed—but then he had the security of a solid, dependable department behind him. The finest police department in the world, he had often declared—and believed in his heart that in doing so he was making no idle boast.

But now he knew that he could no longer depend on it; knew that disloyalty and crookedness were at work within it. Knew that at least some of those men on whose integrity he would have staked his life had sold him out....

It was the night on which John Wenzel died in his cell that had brought that bitter realization home to the commissioner.

Wenzel had been in good health when he entered that cell, and little more than an hour later he had been found writhing on the floor, dying a horrible death. In some seemingly incredible way the Blazing Eye had reached him right there.

To Stanley Kirkpatrick there could be only one answer to

that mystery. He had had the cell searched, had had the entire cell block examined from end to end—but no trace of the death-dealing apparatus was found. Then it must have been there and been taken away....

"Who was in that cell since Wenzel was locked in it?" he had asked. "Who came to see him?"

Wenzel had had only one visitor, was the answer—Detective Albert Geiger, of the Chinatown Squad. Geiger had come in to question Wenzel about fifteen minutes before the restaurant man's withered body was discovered on the floor. Geiger—a man with an excellent record; but Kirkpatrick had put a tail on him immediately, had instructed the shadow to call headquarters and notify him of the first suspicious circumstance that developed.

Besides the man who was shadowing Geiger, Kirkpatrick had assigned others of his most dependable men to investigate the activities of the Chinatown squad. That was last night—and in twenty-four hours they had turned up evidence that could lead to only one conclusion: the whole squad had been corrupted— had been "reached" by the master of the Blazing Eye!

That was a galling admission for Stanley Kirkpatrick to have to make. It gave him no peace, no rest, preyed on his mind every moment. Suddenly he found himself like a lost man, with nowhere to turn, nothing on which he could depend with any security. How far, he asked himself again and again, had this corruption eaten? How many of his men were disaffected?

If only there was something to fight! If only he had proof of Geiger's double-dealing, could confront him with it....

Kirkpatrick sat at his desk shortly after eight-thirty that

night, grimly mapping what he would do if that evidence came into his hands, when the telephone rang. The voice of Delehanty, the tail he had put on Geiger, came to him over the wire.

"I have what you want, Commissioner," he announced tersely. "If you will meet me as soon as possible I can prove it to you."

Stanley Kirkpatrick's face was a fiery red as he dropped the instrument into its cradle and shoved back his chair. Out of the top drawer of his desk he took a loaded automatic and slipped it into his pocket—and like a man in a dream he marched out of his office.

IT WAS First Grade Detective Albert Geiger whose sudden appearance caused Blinky McQuade's eyes to widen behind his thick-lensed spectacles. He knew Geiger by sight and by reputation; and what he had heard of the man had led him to expect that Geiger would step into such a rendezvous with guns flaming. But, instead of that, he walked in with a grin; he shook hands with Stud Poker and chatted with the politician—and then leaned over the table where Sam Yarwitz was working over his roll, organizing the crews that would tear lower New York wide open on the morrow.

Albert Geiger ran his eyes over those names and gave them his endorsement; suggested others that should be added, some that should be switched to work they were better fitted to handle!

Geiger had sold out! He was one of the Genghis Khan organization—and as Wentworth listened he learned that Geiger was not alone. Dozens of his mates had gone bad with him! The force of which Stanley Kirkpatrick was so proud had developed a cancer that was eating the strength out of it—just as it would eat the heart out of him when he discovered it!

Now, Wentworth realized, it would be useless to go to the commissioner with what he had discovered. Now Kirkpatrick was hamstrung, helpless. Now the responsibility for saving New York from the demoralizing catastrophe that threatened it was the Spider's alone!

"Good work!" Geiger clapped Yarwitz on the back. "Guess you've taken care of about everything—but if anything goes wrong, you know where to look for me. I'll be there in one-fifty when the big parade goes by. Be seeing you all—in church!" he grinned, as he started for the stairway.

But before his broad-shouldered figure had faded into the darkness his echoing footsteps suddenly stopped. For an instant he stood there—and then he whirled.

"Stand where you are, Geiger!" a crisp voice snapped in the sudden stillness—the voice of Police Commissioner Stanley Kirkpatrick!

Geiger paid no heed. Whirling on his heel, he raced back toward the gangsters, his snarling face apoplectic.

"The commissioner!" he rasped. "Get him, you mugs! Out with that light—and let him have it!"

Through the empty loft a police whistle shrilled, and the pound of feet seemed to come from all directions. Kirkpatrick was not alone; he had brought a squad with him.

"The cops!" one of the panicky thugs yelled as the lights went out, and instantly chairs were overturned and flung across the floor as the hoodlums bolted toward the stairs, the windows, any way of escape.

But escape was not for Albert Geiger. He was desperate. Kirkpatrick had recognized him, and the commissioner's death seemed to promise his only security. Crouching behind the desk at which Stud Poker had sat, he waited with his gun in one hand, his flashlight in the other.

Wentworth glimpsed him in the dim light from an arc light outside a dirty window, just as he was about to follow Deacon Baumgarten to safety. Geiger's gun was up, ready, his finger set to flash on the light. Kirkpatrick was coming running across the floor, almost on top of him—a target that he could not miss.

It was too late for Wentworth to draw and fire; too late to do anything but fling himself at the renegade and knock the light out of his hand just as it flashed on. Geiger's gun roared harmlessly. Together they went down, battling furiously on the floor. But suddenly the desperate detective broke loose and started to run.

At that moment one of Kirkpatrick's men found a dangling light bulb and switched it on—and Geiger was brought down by a hail of bullets before he could reach the stairway.

Blinky McQuade sprang to his feet and tried to dart to safety at the same instant, but before he had gone half a dozen steps he was surrounded by leveled guns. Scowling blackly, he raised his hands and surrendered, to be joined a few minutes later by six others who had been rounded up by the police. Six thugs who had not been as fast as their leaders—but Pokashefsky, Yarwitz and the Deacon had made good their escape, Wentworth noticed. The devilment would go on without these nobodies, without Albert Geiger.

Something of that must have run through Stanley Kirkpatrick's mind as he stood over the badly wounded detective and eyed him bitterly.

"I'm afraid you won't be on hand tomorrow, Geiger," he clipped; "and your pals in the department won't be on hand either. I am switching the entire detail tomorrow; bringing in men from Brooklyn and Queens to take over the lower city until we can determine how many here in Manhattan have sold out with you."

THAT WAS all Blinky heard before he was bundled into a patrol wagon with the others and carted off to a cell—to sit on the edge of his cot for long hours trying to figure a way out of his quandary. To reveal his identity to Kirkpatrick would be to betray his carefully built up Blinky McQuade personality and ruin its future effectiveness—and yet he had to get out of that cell; had to find a way of circumventing the Blazing Eye before noon the next day.

Reluctantly he was forced to the conclusion that there was no other way than to take Kirkpatrick into his confidence—but when he tried to get word to the commissioner the jailer laughed at him. Blocked in that attempt, he could only wait for arraignment in the morning. Perhaps Pokashefsky would have a bondsman on hand to bail them out; or, if not, Wentworth would be able to appeal to the judge to communicate with Kirkpatrick.

But there was no arraignment in the morning.

Wentworth watched the hours go past. Nine, ten, ten-thirty,

eleven—and he realized that the commissioner was keeping these prisoners hidden away, unbooked; was taking the law into his own hands until after this crisis was past. And then it would be too late!

At eight-thirty the guard had brought breakfast, but he had been alert; had given Wentworth no slightest opportunity for a break. But he must make an opportunity; must fight his way out of there without delay!

But how?

To feign sickness might bring a police doctor—but probably not for several hours; and now minutes were infinitely precious. Sickness would not work, but death….

The guard had resolved to pay no more attention to that troublesome old coot with the glasses. The fellow must be a nut, he decided—trying to get them to call the commissioner for him! Just a nut. But when he heard a gurgling groan come from the direction of Blinky's cell, he listened—and then sped down the corridor.

The nut was trying to bump himself off! There he was, his belt around his neck, hanging from the top of his cell!

The guard took one look at Blinky's bulging eyes, at his protruding tongue—and he had the cell door unlocked, was inside, lifting the taut body to take the weight off the neck. And for that kindly office he received a clout on the back of the head that sent him spinning. Across the cell he reeled—and before he could catch his breath McQuade, miraculously free of the belt that had been strangling him, was upon him, choking him and hammering him into unconsciousness.

That was necessary, Wentworth regretted. He made it as painless as possible; knocked the man out with a clean blow to the jaw, and then stripped off his uniform, to don it on top of his own shabby garments. Safe in that disguise, he stepped out of the cell, walked down the corridor and cautiously made his way out of the building.

Eleven forty-five! Only fifteen minutes left!

In the men's room of a bar he stripped off the keeper's uniform and then hurried out to hail a cab. Just what form this latest outrage of the Blazing Eye would take he did not know, but it would be perpetrated somewhere along lower Broadway, along Ben Waldo's route to City Hall. One place was probably as likely as another—but Albert Geiger had said that he would be at one-fifty. One-fifty Broadway, that meant.

Wentworth told the driver to take him to that address, but the lower city was already traffic-congested because of the approaching procession. The taxi had to detour; seemed to crawl along, and the minutes were speeding past. Trinity's bell was sounding the noon hour when he got out and ran to the doorway of 150 Broadway!

The procession would be along at any moment, and now where should he turn? Grasping anywhere for a suggestion, he ran his eyes over the building directory on the lobby wall—and found his answer. One name in the scores listed there fairly leaped out at him.

Trueman Harmon—investment broker!

That might be a coincidence, of course—but Wentworth raced for the elevator and asked for the sixth floor. Six hundred was the number of the Harmon suite—at the front of the building, as he had expected. What he would do when he got in there he did not know. Enough to get inside—to have a look at those front windows over Broadway....

He started toward the door warily—and then froze in his tracks as the door of the office next to Harmon's opened. Out of it came Ansel Alden and four of Penozzi's thugs! Straight across the corridor they walked—and into Harmon's office!

WENTWORTH'S BRAIN raced with lightning speed at that moment. In a flash he was at the door of the office from which Alden had just come. It was unlocked. He stepped inside, found the office unoccupied, furnished with nothing but a desk, a wardrobe and a few chairs. Instantly the emergency make-up materials which he kept sewed in the collar of his coat and the cuffs of his trousers were out and on the desk; his flying fingers were at work on his face, stripping off the Blinky McQuade disguise and creating the ugly, terrifying visage of the Spider.

Out from beneath the lining of Blinky's ragged coat came a black cape and a limp felt hat—and the Spider was ready. Clutching the revolver he had taken from the jail guard, he stepped out of the office and into the one across the corridor.

The moment he stepped inside that door one of Penozzi's thugs reached out to grab him—but Wentworth's gun was already swinging down. It caught the fellow across the temple and knocked him limp. Snatching up the weapon that fell from the thug's hand, Wentworth sprinted across the little reception room and into the main office—where a dozen clerks and stenographers sat bound and gagged on the floor against the wall; where Alden and his four companions were just about to open the door of Harmon's private office, which extended across the front of the building.

Alden's hand was on the knob, the killers were ready with drawn guns beside him—when they whirled in astonishment. That astonishment was their doom. Their guns came up instinctively—but before they could fire the office rocked with a crackle of shots that seemed to come from a machine gun! They went down almost simultaneously, all five of them, so speedily did Wentworth's deadly guns roar their message of death.

No time now for nice, merciful, disabling shooting. The fate of a city was at stake. The Spider shot point-blank, shot to kill, shot to blast them out of his way so that he could hurl himself at that door and plunge into the front office—where five Orientals who crouched at the open window turned to meet him.

Even as the door opened, a knife snaked across the room and embedded itself in the wood—a knife that would have pierced Wentworth's throat if the opening door had not intervened.

Wentworth's first bullet caught the thrower and dropped him to the floor. His second drilled a gleaming-toothed Hindu through the forehead—and then his triggers clicked without result. His guns were empty—but still good as missiles. One of them landed squarely in the face of a Chinese who leaped at him; and the other—

The other he clutched like a club and flung himself at the two Orientals who still occupied the window. Leaped at them like a madman—for now his eardrums throbbed with the stirring notes of one of Sousa's marches. The procession was downstairs;

the band was right in front of the building—and those devils were crouching over a machine that looked like an electric coffee grinder, a machine with a round spout that was trained on a spot in the middle of the street… a spot over which Waldo's car would have to pass!

The gay notes of the march and the bedlam of cheers that welled up from thousands of throats drove Wentworth berserk. One of the Orientals leaped at him with a knife, but his heavy revolver came down so hard that it crashed through the fellow's skull—and caught there! Releasing his grip on its butt, he threw himself bare-handed at the other man and hauled him away from that death-machine.

Savagely he pummeled the fierce-eyed Jap—but the fellow whipped at him with the metal box that had covered the death-machine and knocked him off his feet. Stunned, his head spinning, Wentworth was on his feet again in a flash and was at the Jap's throat, dragging him away from within reach of the murderous mechanism.

Breast to breast they struggled just behind the window— and through it Wentworth caught a glimpse of Waldo's car approaching. Smiling and wholly unconscious of danger, the flyer was waving to the cheering crowd. Suddenly new strength seemed to surge through Wentworth; strength that enabled him to lift the Jap bodily and hurl him out of the window!

The Spider was after him in a flash. Out onto the ledge he sprang and held up his hands for silence.

"Get back, Waldo!" he yelled, as horrified silence gripped that

154

portion of the thronged street "Get out of that car before you are killed! Out, man—go on, out!"

The driver jammed his foot on the brakes, and Waldo, puzzled, put his legs over the back and dropped to the pavement.

"The rest of you—get off Broadway!" the Spider megaphoned to them through his cupped hands. "The Blazing Eye is all around you! The Blazing Eye—"

Before he could get any farther, the burning death struck. From a score of different windows along Broadway those infernal death-machines stabbed out at the throngs on the sidewalks—stabbed at invisible marks that must have been painted there during the night to attract their deadly currents. Scream and shrieks rent the air as the stricken and terrified victims rushed madly in every direction—but the police had heard and understood the Spider's warning.

"Get off Broadway! Into the side streets or the buildings!" Powerful amplifiers relayed his message up and down the street—and the crowd melted away, to leave Broadway as deserted as the street of a ghost town.

Wentworth waited for no more. Springing back into the office, he sped through the outer office—and glanced down at Alden as he passed. The man was still conscious but had not long to live. Wentworth stooped and lifted him, carrying him through the reception room into the hallway and across to the office on the other side. Quickly he locked the door and then bent over the dying man.

"Where do you figure in this, Alden?" he urged, as he tried to make the explorer comfortable on the floor. "Still trying to get your hands on the Genghis Khan rubies?"

"No—that was a bluff—a cover," Alden barely managed to whisper. "There is something far more valuable at stake—a tremendous fortune—the loot the Blazing Eye is accumulating. I wanted to elbow in on that—wanted to muscle in on the Genghis Khan role—that Dillon Harmon is getting away with."

"Dillon Harmon—are you sure?"

Wentworth bent dose and pressed his ear to the barely moving lips.

"Of course," Ansel Alden husked. "He put it—over on you—last—night. Fooled you—just like he—fooled—every...."

That was where death silenced him.

CHAPTER 10
DOOMED GARDEN

THE PANICKY terror that gripped Broadway and then the wild battle with Stud Poker's army of thieves that followed close on its heels kept the police so occupied that they had time for no more than superficial search of the sixth floor of 150 Broadway. When they unlocked the door of the unoccupied office next to Trueman Harmon's suite they found only another corpse to add to the collection the Harmon offices had yielded—the half-stripped corpse of Ansel Alden.

Had they bothered to open the window and climb out onto the ledge that ran along the side of the building, they would have discovered Richard Wentworth there, clad in Alden's clothing, all trace of the Spider's ugly visage removed. But they did not look there, as Wentworth had been reasonably sure that they would not.

Ten minutes after they had gone, he let himself back through the window and cautiously looked out into the now quiet hallway; and half an hour later he was back in Sutton Place, waiting for the call that he was certain would come from Stanley Kirkpatrick. It did—within minutes after he arrived. Kirkpatrick invited him to come down to headquarters.

Wentworth obliged promptly. Immaculate as always in a well-tailored suit of his own clothing, he arrived at the commissioner's office as quickly as a taxicab could speed him to headquarters.

"What is it, Kirk—got your hands on the Blazing Eye?" he greeted as he came through the doorway.

For a moment the commissioner regarded him quizzically.

"No, Dick," he said then, with a sigh that was a mixture of admiration and resignation. "I wish we had. But we have plenty of other news." Again he paused and looked at Wentworth with the expression of one who feels that he is telling a story that the listener already knows. "We have gotten hold of one of the death-machines the Blazing Eye uses for his deviltry—thanks to the Spider.

"We have a dozen of the best scientists in the city working on it now, and we already know pretty much what it is about. As you suspected, it is a type of ray-projector—one that fairly sets the blood on fire. It raises the body temperature to such a degree that the tissues are burned up. Once the blood is so affected, there seems to be no cure; it goes on boiling until the body is utterly wasted away—as we have seen too often.

"So far as we have been able to discover, the rays need a magnetic pole toward which they must be directed. That is the reason for those phosphorescent eyes of which we have been hearing so much. They were the attraction—but the contact, strange to say, is better completed when the rays first pass through a human body. That is why a victim does not even have to stand directly between the eye and the machine—these diabolical rays actually reach out to clutch him!

"The man who perfected that contraption is a scientist or an inventor of the first water—a man who might use his brains to so much better advantage," Kirkpatrick deplored. "He almost succeeded in slaughtering thousands of people on lower Broadway this noon—"

"Yes, I know—the radio carried a very dramatic account of it," Wentworth nodded. "Waldo seems to have had a narrow escape."

"But the radio did not mention that we have discovered that the sidewalks down there were practically covered with this ray-attracting mixture," Kirkpatrick added. "Not phosphorescent. This was transparent. A solution that must have been applied to them last night—and that would have taken untold thousands of lives today if it had not been for a miracle."

"A miracle performed by the Spider," Wentworth reminded, and Stanley Kirkpatrick nodded willing confirmation.

"By the Spider," he admitted. "He succeeded where the police department failed."

No man knew better than Wentworth what it cost Kirkpatrick to make that admission. Knowing what his friend had discovered and endured, his heart went out to him. Had he been able to change Stanley Kirkpatrick and remold him at that moment, he would have transformed him not an iota; not even his bulldogged insistence on his own ideas and his own way of doing things, not even his unyielding opposition to the ways of the Spider—for Stanley Kirkpatrick was exactly the sort of man New York City needed for its police commissioner.

"We were saved today—but that is not the answer," Kirkpatrick shook his head. "This is only a reprieve, Dick. The murderer is still at large. Until we have rounded him up, there can be no security for the city—"

The telephone interrupted him, and for an instant the commissioner's eyes met Wentworth's—eyes that silently said, "I told you so." He listened intently, and his fingers drummed nervously on the top of his desk as the voice of one of his men came to him from Madison Square Garden—a voice that was tense with excitement.

"There are at least half a dozen of them here, Commissioner," the detective reported. "Chinks and Japs and one Hindu we've spotted. We've been watching them like hawks—and just now we collared a Jap in gray coat and cap like the hot-dog and soda-pop sellers. He was carrying a hot-dog oven—but when we opened it we found it contained some sort of a machine. He fought like hell to get away, but—"

Abruptly the words ended in a gasp—and then an agonized scream came over the wire; a scream that faded and was lost in the scraping sounds of a body sliding to the bottom of a telephone booth.

"There it is," Kirkpatrick faced Wentworth grimly. "That was Ed Hubert—from Madison Square Garden. You know what is going on up there—the public reception and entertainment for Waldo. The murdering devils are still after him. They are carting their death-machines into the Garden—where more than fifteen thousand people will be jammed within an hour!"

Wentworth waited for no more. He was already out of his chair, starting for the door as the commissioner grabbed the phone and barked an order for his car.

SWIFTLY THE machine carved a way through traffic as it sped them uptown—and as it went the two silent men in the rear visualized the appalling possibilities that lay ahead of them. If the walls of the Garden had been coated with that ray-attracting mixture and the demoniacal machines went to work when every seat was filled—

The master of the Blazing Eye was a genius of the first water, Wentworth admitted; a perverted genius who brought to crime a thoroughness and foresight that made him a terrible menace. Like an expert chess-player, he had laid out his diabolical plan move after move, overlooking no possibility, capping each chance of failure with a blow that would be even more staggering than the one which misfired. A warped-minded genius who must be apprehended and killed before his mad dream brought misery and death to thousands of victims not only in New York but throughout the nation....

The police had removed Ed Hubert's body and roped off

the area around the telephone booth in which he had died, when Wentworth and Kirkpatrick arrived at the Garden; but his assailant had not been apprehended. A long knife, plunged deep into his back, had ended Hubert's life, but the killer had slipped away in the crowd—was loose somewhere there inside the packed auditorium, ready to continue his murderous role on a grand scale.

"How to find one man in this crowd!" Kirkpatrick groaned, as they went inside and looked around the great building, filled from floor to ceiling with tier after tier of close-packed humanity. "How to find a hundred killers here—and there may be that many!"

There might be that many, Wentworth agreed—and there might be just a handful. If the Orientals had been at work in there beforehand, had coated the walls or seats with their devilish preparation, one or two of the death-ray machines would be sufficient to spread doom on every side. But where could those machines be concealed?

Somewhere central, certainly. Somewhere that would enable them to sweep all sides of the building from top to bottom.

In the center of the arena was the platform where Ben Waldo sat, surrounded by the members of the reception committee and public officials who had been invited to join him there. On that platform—or perhaps beneath it? That would enable the ray-operator to sweep the lower tiers, but hardly the upper ones....

"Ben Waldo is no stranger to airplanes," the voice of the chairman boomed out through the loudspeakers, "but I think we have one here today that will interest him. As a special feature

161

of this entertainment we have arranged for a demonstration of what promises to be the airplane of the future—the helicopter! Ladies and gentlemen—I give you the airplane that flies like a hummingbird, at any speed, in any direction, up or down, that stands still in the air. But see for yourselves."

As he finished, a section of the wall at one end of the arena opened and a small plane with overhead rotors rolled out. With a barely audible hum, the motor began to rumble, and then the machine left the ground. Slowly and with perfect ease it took to the air and began to circle the auditorium, making the turns at each end with no difficulty, ranging from the arena floor to the high ceiling—

That was it! Suddenly Wentworth's nerves tingled, and he knew that he had found the answer! The helicopter—it had complete range of the Garden; could spread death from tier to tier! That Oriental whom Ed Hubert had caught was only a blind, a decoy to keep the police searching the tiers for death-machines—while destruction came from the air!

It must be stopped! But how? How could he possibly reach it, up there in the air?

"That plane—there's your answer, Kirk!" he barked at the commissioner. "Try to empty this Garden at once—there may still be time; but I doubt it. I am going to stop the thing—somehow!"

Already an idea had dawned upon him; a desperate plan was taking form in his whirling brain. Leaving Kirkpatrick, he ran out of the auditorium, back to the general manager's office.

"This is police business!" he snapped at that surprised individual. "You're going to have people dying by the thousands inside there in a few minutes—unless I can prevent it. I want to get up into the rafters, the crossbeams above the ceiling. Quick—how do I reach them?"

The manager started to sputter questions, but Wentworth had him by the arm, was dragging him from the office, forcing him to lead the way to the level of the top balcony—and then above that by a spindly stairway that gave way to a thin metal ladder. **THAT WAS** as far as the manager would go. Beyond that Wentworth was on his own, picking his way with his flashlight amid a wilderness of girders and braces, along narrow catwalks that ran from girder to girder and spider-webbed the auditorium just below the roof. Beneath that metal network was the Garden ceiling, a blue reproduction of the night heaven, with electric stars peeping through.

Out over the center of the ceiling he made his way, and there found one of the numerous trapdoors that could be lifted to afford a view of the auditorium. Everything still seemed to be all right down there—and for a moment he feared that he was wrong; feared that he had jumped at a conclusion that would make him appear ridiculous—if it did not plunge the crowded Garden into a fatal panic....

But only for a moment—and then he knew that his fears were all too well-founded!

As he lifted the trap and stared down at the smoke-hazed auditorium, the lights suddenly went out—and in their place, great, almond-shaped eyes blazed with a cold, phosphorescent light from every corner of the building! Scores of eyes—from every tier! Suddenly the great auditorium had been transformed into a Stygian pit—the pit of the Blazing Eye!

For a long, shocked moment there was complete silence; a hushed silence that seemed to clutch every throat; a silence disturbed only by the low hum of the circling helicopter. And then the silence was shattered, pierced by a shrill scream that seemed to let loose a bedlam that was earsplitting.

The Blazing Eye had struck! The helicopter had opened up with its deadly ray-projectors and was spreading doom on every side!

Grim-eyed and tight-lipped, Wentworth clutched the edges of the trap and stared down at the slaughter that he was powerless to prevent. In the reflected light of the phosphorescent eyes he could now distinguish the milling crowd; thousands of people who looked like weird creatures from another world, fighting and tearing at one another as they struggled frantically to escape, shrinking back in abject terror whenever the silver-gray bulk of the helicopter approached and hovered above them!

That machine was a terrible weapon in the hands of these inhuman murderers. Like a great insect, it hung almost stationary in the air, while it poured its deadly sting into its helpless victims....

But Kirkpatrick had not been idle since Wentworth left him. He had made his way to the center of the arena, to the platform, and now stood before the microphone.

"Get down on the floor!" his voice roared through the amplifiers. "Get behind your seats and creep out on your stomachs!

Don't stand up—and don't lose your heads! Steady, men—steady! Down on the floor!"

The wild panic seemed to rage on unabated, but now Wentworth saw that those calming words were beginning to have their effect. Many were obeying. In a few minutes the seats were half-emptied and the uproar was diminishing as desperation forced calmness upon the trapped victims.

The inhuman devils in the helicopter realized that, too—and promptly moved to check it. Like a darting hornet, the machine sped toward the middle of the Garden and hovered over the platform—which was just the opportunity Richard Wentworth had been waiting for.

Down through the trap he let himself, to hang by his fingers until the machine was just beneath him—and then he let go.

Like a parachute jumper during the first few moments before his 'chute opens, he shot through the air, his eyes riveted on the silver-gray hulk beneath him—and then, before the fiendish occupants had any inkling of what was happening, he was upon them; had crashed squarely into the helicopter's cockpit. There were three Orientals in the roomy gondola, one at the controls and two operating the death-ray projectors. One of them was beneath Wentworth when he struck; went down in a limp, broken-necked heap under him as the machine pitched wildly and threatened to get out of control.

Shaken and half-stunned, his breath almost knocked out of him, Wentworth staggered to his feet just as a knife sliced through the side of his arm and a beady-eyed Chinese crouched over him, to knock him back to the floor. Desperately Wentworth grabbed for the fellow and tried to swing at him with an automatic, but the Oriental was like a cat. He was out of reach instantly, then was closing in again—and now the pilot had left the controls and was coming in also, a gleaming knife in his hand.

From front and back they were coming at him in that little cockpit that barely gave him space to move. He could not hope to avoid them both; knew that they must surely down him, unless—

He flattened himself on the floor and dived forward, to squirm between the pilot's legs and upset him—and then to wriggle past. Instantly the fellow was back on his feet and the other was beside him. Wentworth felt a knife plunge into his back, felt something come down on his head with sickening force—again and again.

But he seemed to feel no pain. Nothing mattered; nothing that they did to him was of any importance. Now he had only one mission—to pound and smash at those controls with his automatic. Only one mission—to put that murder plane out of action; to send it crashing to the floor of the Garden.

Glass smashed, wires tore loose, delicate controls were battered into unrecognizable junk, the control board lights went out—and then Wentworth felt himself falling… falling… Was it he or was it the helicopter? How could he tell? Everything was rushing past him, the whole world seemed to be turned up at a crazy angle—and then it all ended in a blinding, all-consuming flash of white light….

IT WAS hours later before Wentworth came back to his

senses; nearly six o'clock when he sat up in a hospital bed and looked at his wristwatch. His head was thick and muggy, his senses dulled—and he knew that he must have been drugged. But there seemed to be nothing more the matter with him. Nothing but a few scratches—that knife wound in his arm and another in his back.

Carefully he stretched his limbs. They were sound and unbroken, and his bandaged wounds gave him no trouble. He got out of bed and experienced only a slight dizziness that went away as he paced up and down the room and called for a nurse.

"Give me my clothes—I'm getting out of here," he announced, and was prepared for the storm of protest that followed.

Wentworth stormed as vigorously as the nurse and doctors, stormed until Kirkpatrick came to see him.

"You ought to stay in bed, Dick," he urged. "You escaped by a miracle when you crashed that helicopter to the Garden floor, but those knife wounds are ugly. You need rest, and this is a good place to get it. I tried to get Nita to come here to you—"

"Nita—where is she?" Wentworth clipped.

"I don't know, Dick," Kirkpatrick was uneasy. "She isn't at home, and your place doesn't answer—"

Sutton Place did not answer! And Nita had not come to him at the hospital—although the radio must have broadcast news of what had occurred in Madison Square Garden. There was only one answer to that—something had happened at Sutton Place; something that made it impossible for Nita to come to his bedside!

"I am leaving here, Kirk—even if I have to go as I am," Wentworth announced with flat finality; and Kirkpatrick nodded helplessly.

"All right," he yielded. "But I am going with you. I am taking you home to Sutton Place and tucking you in bed, understand that."

Kirkpatrick went home with Wentworth, but he did not tuck him into bed—for the moment they stepped into the Sutton Place living room all thought of retiring was dashed from their minds.

Wentworth's uneasiness increased when he entered his grounds by way of the side-street gate and saw that the building on the water's edge was dark from top to bottom. Fear tentacles wove about him and filled him with dread premonitions as he led the way to the elevator and then stepped out into the third-floor foyer.

Still nobody to greet him and not a sign of life. Now he knew that there was something wrong. Anxiously he stepped to the living room door and opened it, stepped back to let Kirkpatrick enter—and suddenly grabbed the commissioner and yanked him back, to drag him to the floor!

"The Blazing Eye!" he rasped a warning. "The room is a trap, Kirk—and we almost walked right into it!"

In that fraction of a second he had glimpsed a phosphorescent, almond-shaped eye that blazed down from the side wall—an eye he would not have seen had he not stepped aside to let Kirkpatrick enter first.

The Blazing Eye there in his living room—that meant that

something had happened to Nita and Jackson and the others. Something… and he hardly dared to think what!

Carefully he backed away from the door and led the way across the foyer to another doorway into a little room just off the living room. Cautiously he opened this door and snapped on the light—and instantly his eyes widened in amazement. There, in the doorway that connected the anteroom with the living room, was one of the death-ray projectors! And, on the floor beside it, lay the unconscious figure of Viola Dunn!

Quickly he disconnected the projector and shoved it out of the doorway, to step into the living room and turn on the lights. By now he was fully prepared for what he would find—but nevertheless he felt his flesh crawl as he stared at the blackened skeleton that lay in the center of the singed hardwood floor.

That ghastly thing was not one of the servants, for they all three sat trussed up helplessly on the floor. Not Jackson or Ram Singh or Jenkyns—but Nita was not there with them!

Cold sweat bathed Wentworth's hands as he tore the gag from between Jackson's distended jaws.

"Miss van Sloan—" he began, but Jackson cut him short.

"She's gone," he groaned. "They took her with them. There is no excuse, sir—not for failing a second time. We thought we were prepared for any sort of an attack—but we never expected them to come down from the roof! They landed there with a plane—a great big helicopter that came down on our tiny sun deck. Before we could help ourselves they had grabbed us one by one—and then they took Miss van Sloan."

"But that thing there on the floor?" Wentworth motioned

toward the macabre skeleton with its encrustation of charred flesh that was all that remained of a human body.

"Hoong Gow," Jackson answered. "They talked to him in Chinese; I couldn't understand—but I guess he got his for falling down on them and not taking care of you the way he was supposed to."

"And Miss Dunn—what is she doing over there in the side room?" Wentworth pressed, as he hurriedly untied Jackson's wrists.

"She was here, talking to Miss van Sloan, when they came in on us," Jackson explained. "They dragged her out of the room, and I don't know what they did with her after that."

But by then Viola Dunn was able to speak for herself. Kirkpatrick had been working over her, chafing her wrists and pouring water down her throat, and he managed to revive her.

"I had come here to try to see you," she groaned when Wentworth questioned her. "I talked to Miss van Sloan—and in the midst of our conversation we were overwhelmed. I tried to stay with Miss van Sloan, but they dragged me away and forced something down my throat that made my senses swim—and that's all I remember."

"Who were they—can you tell us that?" Wentworth asked. "Haven't you any idea where they have taken her?"

"They were just Dillon Harmon's usual gang of mixed Orientals." She shook her head wearily. "I don't know where they came from or where they went—nobody seems to know that but Dillon."

"Dillon Harmon?" Wentworth caught her up quickly. "The last time you were here you suspected Ansel Alden, and now—"

The girl's hot, defiant eyes stopped him.

"That was what I told you then," she admitted bitterly, "but I lied. I came here then under orders—to direct your suspicion against Alden. Who sent me? The man I was going to marry—or thought I was. Dillon Harmon. He was my fiancé—not Peter Ellison. I did just what he told me to do, and as a reward he threw me over—for your Nita van Sloan!"

Kirkpatrick whistled—a soft, amazed whistle.

"The murdering devil has Nita, and he left this death trap to finish you, Dick," he summed up. "And then, to clear his skirts entirely, he left Miss Dunn lying here, drugged, beside the ray-projector, so that she would be found after your death and would be accused of having murdered you!"

CHAPTER 11
BEHIND THE EYE

NITA WAS gone! Wentworth stared long and hard out of the dark window—and knew that nothing else mattered except coming to grips with the fiend who had seized her. Nita was kidnapped, in the hands of the masquerading Genghis Khan, the master of the Blazing Eye—and that was Dillon Harmon!

"Get out the Mercedes, Ram Singh," he ordered. "We are going after the *missie sahib.*"

"I am going with you, Dick," Kirkpatrick said quietly.

That offer Wentworth could not refuse, and when the Mercedes sped through the wall gates and headed for the Queensborough Bridge, Kirkpatrick shared the rear seat with him, while Jackson occupied the front section with Ram Singh at the wheel.

It was Kirkpatrick who spoke first.

"We have to snare him, Dick—we can't fail!" he suddenly voiced the worry that was gnawing at him, the mental torment that had given him no rest for days.

"This morning, just before the attack on lower Broadway, I learned how completely he has covered the city's industries. Every line has received his demands—stores, restaurants, factories, banks, theaters, hotels, the public utilities; every line of business has heard from him or received calls from his crooks.

"Even the trains and busses, the steamship lines. He has threatened that not a train will leave the city, not a boat will be allowed to pass out of the harbor, unless the operating companies meet his demands for tribute."

Poor Kirk! It would have been an easy matter for him to have called headquarters and had the police surround the Harmon home, Wentworth realized. Ordinarily that would have been his procedure—but not tonight. Tonight he had not called on his men—because he did not dare! Kirkpatrick, the stickler for police regularity, could no longer trust his own force!

But now that would end. Wentworth's hard fists clenched and his eyes narrowed as the car left the boulevard and swung into Kew. Leaning forward, he directed Ram Singh to the Harmon mansion, set well back from the road in its ample grounds; had

172

the Sikh drive past it so that they could come back and approach unobserved.

AGAIN THERE were lights in the lower-floor windows, as Wentworth led the way into the grounds, and again he kept to the bushes—but this time they were challenged before they were halfway to the building. Out of the darkness a shadowy figure suddenly loomed and barked an unintelligible question, to follow it with a shot before they could answer.

Instantly that report was echoed by another and another, by six orange flashes in the darkness—a ring of gunmen that intervened between them and the building. Then Wentworth caught a new sound—stealthy footsteps creeping up on them. The gunmen were closing in, trying to surround them.

"Back!" he called softly to Jackson, who was nearest to him. "Back and stay together. Don't let them separate us. Pass the word to the others."

But before Jackson could obey, a light suddenly blazed out of the night a few yards from them—a powerful flashlight that lit up an area more than a hundred feet square. Kirkpatrick's police flash! And caught full in its beam was a scarred-faced Chinese who had half-risen from behind a clump of shrubbery.

Kirkpatrick's gun blazed almost the instant his light flashed on. The Oriental straightened, seemed to rise off the ground, to stand on tiptoes before his knees buckled under him and pitched him forward on his face. And before his body hit the ground the guns of his companions roared again—but this time their vengeful aim was centered behind the easy mark of that glowing flashlight.

Kirkpatrick was hit. With a half-smothered groan he staggered backward, and Wentworth caught him in his arms, lowered him gently to the turf as he whirled to snake forward and blast sudden death at those hidden ambushers.

Seething rage gripped Wentworth as he crept forward. Twice he fired at a patch of darkness blacker than the rest of the night, and twice a scream of pain rewarded him—but now the hidden Orientals no longer returned his fire. They seemed to have withdrawn, seemed to have retreated to the house.

"Slowly," Wentworth husked a warning to Jackson and Ram Singh. "This may be a trick to lead us on."

Cautiously they edged closer, the faint noise of their creeping the only sound in the still night—until suddenly they heard the roar of motors, several of them. Headlights flared, and down the drive swept three cars, one after the other. Orange flashes from their windows answered the shots Wentworth triggered at them—and then they were gone, sweeping out of the driveway into the street on screaming tires.

They had made their getaway—and with them had gone Dillon Harmon. Wentworth knew that even before he entered the silent house. With Jackson and Ram Singh carrying Kirkpatrick, he led the way. The living room in which he had battled the Penozzi mobsters was empty, and so was room after room on the lower floor. The lights were still lit, half-emptied plates of sandwiches stood on the tables, half-smoked cigarettes lay on ashtrays—but Dillon Harmon and his Oriental escort were gone.

The house was empty—until he stepped into a little room at

one side of the building. It was dark, until he felt for the light button and switched it on, to reveal what appeared to be a den or a study that now was in the wildest disarray. Bookcases had been emptied and overturned, a large desk had been cleared of its drawers and upended, a safe stood with gaping door and emptied compartments—everything had been dumped in the middle of the floor; and in the midst of the litter and wreckage lay the blood-covered figure of a man!

Wentworth bent over him and extricated him from the mess, lifted him to the only chair that still stood upright. A ghastly-faced man whom he recognized as Trueman Harmon!

"Mr. Harmon—" he pressed close to the half-dead investment broker—"what happened? Who did this to you?"

Harmon's skull was broken, his face deluged with blood, and his chest, bared of coat and shirt, was a ghastly horror of cuts and stabs. He had been tortured so horribly that it was amazing that he still lived—and yet he managed to move his blood-gummed lips; managed to find strength for a last few words.

"My gem collection," he gasped. "They thought I kept it here—tried to make me show them—where. It was those Genghis Khan rubies—all my fault—for wanting them—"

"Then you are the one who commissioned Morton Cramer to get them for you?" Wentworth began to understand.

"Yes—and the bloody stones are cursed," Harmon husked. "There has been trouble—nothing but trouble—ever since. They brought thieves swarming around me—and they drove Dillon mad—turned him into a murdering maniac—a creature who must be killed—"

175

"Dillon—your son?" Wentworth rallied him when the gasping voice was almost stilled.

"My son," the old man repeated. "It is not his fault—the stones—they made him do it—crazed him—made him a criminal—a murderer—the Blazing Eye. And now he even let his killers have me—so that I could not talk.

"He is getting away—tonight—New York—"

With that the last flicker of life winked out, and the tortured body found relief, the harassed brain found peace....

Ansel Alden, Viola Dunn, and now Trueman Harmon, his own father—all had placed the guilt for the Blight of the Blazing Eye at Dillon Harmon's door; and now the man had made his escape!

THE COMMISSIONER'S wounds were bad but not serious, and Ram Singh had dressed them as expertly as a nurse. Kirkpatrick needed to be taken to a hospital, but waiting a few minutes more would do him no harm—and that house still might hold secrets that would prove invaluable.

Quickly Wentworth hurried to the second floor and scouted through the rooms—until he located the three that were Dillon Harmon's personal suite. The rooms were upset, closets and bureau drawers half-open, a half-filled suitcase forgotten on one of the chairs. Dillon Harmon, it was evident, had left in a hurry—and in his haste he had neglected to dispose of several items of damning significance.

From the depths of a clothes closet Wentworth hauled two of the death-ray projectors. From a locked desk drawer which he broke open he took a sheaf of the Blazing Eye's rice-paper death

176

warnings. And among a number of discarded trinkets that had been tossed into a wastebasket was a curiously-wrought serpent ring which he had often seen on the finger of Moo Fong....

Moo Fong! A twinge of guilt coursed through Wentworth as he recalled his vow to the dying Chinaman whose last blinked-out words had served to save hundreds from death. Moo Fong still was unavenged, and now his murderer had added the kidnapping of Nita van Sloan to his criminal score—and was at that very moment making good his escape!

Bitter disappointment and discouragement, a sense of utterly hopeless futility, weighed heavily on Wentworth's shoulders as he went back downstairs and gave the word to start for Manhattan.

Dillon Harmon was gone. The blackness of the night had swallowed him up—and intuition whispered to Wentworth that this was the end; that the Blazing Eye had reached the end of his course in New York and was making a getaway. A getaway that would mean the doom of Nita van Sloan....

Like a caged tiger he paced the living room of his apartment and stared out into that all-enveloping darkness, after Kirkpatrick had been safely delivered at a hospital. Somewhere, under cover of that blanket of darkness, Nita was a helpless prisoner, hoping against hope that he would come to her rescue before—

Somewhere in that blackness there must be a clue. Someone must know where she had been taken; must know where to locate this hell-spawned master of the Blazing Eye. Someone....

Suddenly he seemed to see clearly through the darkness; to look into a bare little chapel where fascinated worshipers stared up at a picture of Genghis Khan that glared down at them with blazing eyes. The chapel of the Blazing Eye! There he would find men who knew how to contact their master; men who would speak even if he had to wring the words from their lips!

Blinky McQuade would be able to succeed where Richard Wentworth and the Spider had failed—and three-quarters of an hour later Blinky shuffled out.

THE MOMENT he left his shabby doorway he knew that he was stepping into an underworld that was transformed since last he had been in it. From the window of the taxi that sped him downtown he had seen plenty of evidence of that change.

Police sirens, speeding squad cars, gangs of thugs pillaging stores, fighting crowds, the bark of shots and the roar of enraged mobs—all had told him that the lid was off; the underworld had snapped its last restraint and was taking the law in its own hands, as Stanley Kirkpatrick had feared would happen. The Blazing Eye had let down the bars and unloosed a deluge that threatened to sweep over the entire city!

The Genghis Khan worshipers would have a directing hand in this! But when Blinky arrived at their chapel, the place was dark. Nothing daunted, he went through the tenement building hallway to the back yard and broke into the place through a window. With his flashlight he searched the back rooms, the chapel itself—and again he sensed that indefinable air of permanent desertion.

Failure....

From there he headed for the coffee pot that was Deacon Baumgarten's headquarters. The Deacon was not there, nor was he to be found in any of the crowded rendezvous Wentworth visited. He seemed to have dropped out of sight since he was last seen several hours ago—entering the chapel.

Suddenly another possible place to try sprang into his mind—the address to which the taxi driver had taken Carlo Penozzi when Wentworth liberated the gangster from Sutton Place. That proved to be a four-story building, the headquarters of a Lithuanian club. The place was dark, and he started to turn away from it—when a sudden hunch stopped him, sent him back to the door; a sudden hunch that was occasioned by the sight of several dark spots on the sidewalk just in front of the door.

Wentworth bent over them, examined them closely. His suspicion had been correct. Those spots were blood!

In a few moments his skeleton key had manipulated the lock, and he stepped into the hall. Here a dim light was burning, but the place was utterly still—until he caught a faint sound that came from somewhere below. The basement, probably… A sound like the closing of a door.

Cautiously he made his way to a stairway that led down; cat-footed his way to the lower floor. There another dim light illuminated the corridor, but at the rear end a stronger light came through the transom over a closed door. Quickly he glanced along the hallway and spied a folding ladder against one of the walls.

Noiselessly he padded to it, put it into position beside the door and mounted to the third step—to peer through the grimy transom at a sight that set his nerves a-tingle!

Carlo Penozzi was in there with ten or twelve of his thugs.

They were grouped around five straight-backed chairs on which sat Deacon Baumgarten and four Orientals. Bound and helpless, the battered and bruised prisoners regarded their captors with set faces and stony eyes—all except two of the Orientals who sagged in their bonds, their heads on their blood-stained chests. Unconscious or dead, Wentworth could not tell which.

"That's the way we do it, see, Deacon?" Penozzi snarled, as he turned from the second of those figures and faced Baumgarten. "Those are pretty tough babies. Think you can stand what they took? Well, you're gonna get every bit of it and worse—unless you talk. I wanta know where you were takin' those bags of dough." He jerked his head toward two satchels that stood open on a table. "There's enough in them for a starter—but it's chicken feed compared to this Genghis Khan's haul. Where is he, Deacon?" he demanded savagely. "Spill it—or start that prayin' you're so good at!"

As he finished he whipped out with a thin-bladed stiletto and slit the Deacon's shirt, cut through his tie, bared his chest to the waist. Again the knife snaked forward—deliberately; but the Deacon had had plenty.

"All right, I'll talk—but it won't do you any good," he snarled. "We were taking them to Pier Forty-two—where the *New York* sails at midnight. At midnight, Penozzi—did you hear that? You can't possibly reach there in time any more."

The *New York!* Wentworth's palms suddenly were clammy, his fingers icy cold. The New York—that was what Trueman Harmon had tried to tell him! Dillon Harmon was making his getaway on the liner *New York,* which would sail from Pier 42 at midnight. Pier 42, on the North River, at the foot of Morton Street—clear across town. It would take at least half an hour to get there—and by then the liner would be out in the bay, on its way to Europe….

CHAPTER 12
EYES OF DEATH

PENOZZI AND his thugs were cursing and wrangling among themselves, were beating up the helpless Deacon— but Wentworth had no time now to go to the man's rescue. His whirling brain was planning madly, desperately. He could not possibly reach Pier 42 in time to catch the liner, but he might be able to catch the vessel after it left the pier! Padding upstairs swiftly, he dashed into the street and ran several blocks until he found a taxi. Leaping through the doorway, he clipped the address of his Sutton Place stronghold—and tossed the driver a ten-dollar bill as a speed bonus.

At last Wentworth leaped out and raced for his gateway, across the grounds and into his doorway, where Ram Singh and Jackson came running to meet him, their eyes wide and questioning.

"The boat!" he clipped, as he headed for the elevator. "We're going out after Nita—taking her off an ocean liner."

Those well-trained servitors needed no other explanation. In the car beside him, they were ready the moment the elevator stopped at the basement level, started on a run along a concrete tunnel that ran out beneath one of the piers on which part of the building stood. At the end of that tunnel was a basin where a powerful-motored little speedboat lay at anchor. Wentworth sprang to the controls, touched a button at the side of the basin—and the end of the pier opened out into the river.

Silently the slim hull slid out into the current, and then the motor opened up and fairly hurled the speedster through the water. That was when Wentworth yielded the wheel to Jackson and stepped back into the little half-cabin, where he pressed a button that swung aside a panel and revealed a lighted make-up mirror and complete kit. Quickly his agile fingers went to work wiping out the last vestige of Blinky McQuade and bringing forth in his stead the ugly, glittering-eyed face of the Spider.

To take Nita from that boat would be no one-man job, Wentworth realized; no job even for a gang—but it was a task which the Spider might be able to accomplish. To rescue Nita and to settle with the Blazing Eye; to unmask him and bring him to justice no matter how many of his Oriental knife-men might surround him—that was the task to which he had committed himself and which he would carry through unless death reached him first....

Quarter past twelve... twenty past... twenty-five... Now they had reached the foot of Manhattan Island—but the *New York* already had passed that point, was heading into the upper bay, approaching the Statue of Liberty. Wentworth sped past South Ferry, swung over toward Governor's Island and then out into the bay.

The speedboat was eating up the distance that separated them from the liner. In a few minutes they would overhaul it, would pull up alongside the dark hull—but suddenly Wentworth's hands tightened on the wheel, his eyes fairly bulged from his head, as he stared at the great statue on Bedloe's Island.

Liberty's torch glowed as usual—but now there were two more lights on the statue! Two great, almond-shaped eyes that blazed out of the floodlight-illumined face! The death sign of the Blazing Eye!

INSTANTLY KIRKPATRICK'S words flashed back into his mind. The master of the Blazing Eye had threatened that no ship would be allowed to leave the harbor unless the steamship company that operated it had met his extortion demands; and now that threat was to be carried out. An example was to be made of the *New York*, its decks swept with terrible death! But the fiendish murderer was on board that vessel himself... He and, presumably, his Oriental cohorts....

For an instant, that nettled Wentworth—and then he knew the answer. The Blazing Eye and his men would know how to protect themselves; they would stay out of reach of the death rays—and when the liner was helpless, its crew and passengers slaughtered, the Orientals would reveal themselves and take it over!

Now the speedboat was abreast of the *New York*, was riding close beside her as Wentworth sought a means of boarding the vessel. There was none—but now the decks above him were crowded with passengers who lined the rails to stare at the blazing-eyed statue. And in them he found his answer. Grabbing a heavy fire extinguisher from the little cabin, he threw it overboard.

"Man overboard! Man overboard!" he shouted wildly, and Jackson and Ram Singh took up his cry.

Almost immediately they were answered. Down from the deck of the liner came several life preservers; one so close that the speedboat was over it in an instant. Seizing the rope attached to it, the Spider "walked" up the side of the hull like the insect whose name he bore.

Hand over hand... until he leaped clear on the deck, a hideous crouching figure from whom the frightened passengers drew back in terror.

"Down—down behind the rails!" he shouted to them, as he flung himself flat on the deck. "Get inside, all of you—into the salons and the companionways—but *creep* there! Those eyes are deadly—the mark of the Blazing Eye that has been terrorizing New York!"

For an instant it seemed that many of them might not believe him—but the sudden screams and shrieks of victims already stricken decided them. Instantly those eager faces disappeared behind the rails and the rush for the inside of the ship began.

But that was only one deck—and there were crowds on all the others. Now Ram Singh and Jackson were over the side. They sped up and down the companionways to the other decks, shouting their warning as they went—but scores of innocent victims were stricken before the alarm reached them.

Darting forward, the Spider leaped up the companionways to the boat deck and then up to the bridge—to hunch in the doorway and confront the startled captain and his officers.

"Your ship is in danger, Captain!" he barked. "There are pirates on board—murderous Orientals who are ready to seize it! Get your men armed and ready before it is too late!"

Before he had finished, the crackle of shots echoed his words; and he knew that Jackson and Ram Singh had clashed with the Orientals, knew that the battle for the possession of the liner had begun. His fingers itched on the triggers of his guns—but he could take no part in that battle. There was something more important waiting for him.

Swinging down from the bridge, he raced to the purser's office and grabbed that astounded officer before he could close his door. The number of Dillon Harmon's cabin he wanted; and in a moment he had it, was racing toward it, his guns blazing at three Orientals who sprang from a passageway and tried to stop him.

Those Orientals died quickly; died with bullet-holes in the center of their foreheads. Past them the Spider leaped, down the short passageway—and into the cabin where Dillon Harmon stood trembling over the berth on which lay Nita's bound figure, bound and half under the effects of a narcotic, Wentworth saw at a glance. His automatic muzzle trained squarely on Harmon's quaking belly.

"Oh, God!" Dillon Harmon gasped, as the color blanched from his face. "Listen to me, Spider—for God's sake, listen to me! This isn't what it seems—it isn't my fault. I had to—"

His eyes were wide and terrified.

That terrified glance had darted in the direction of a curtain-draped closet in the corner of the cabin, Wentworth had noted. As he looked at the curtain now it seemed to sway. The cabin light dimmed to half-power, as the current was shifted from one dynamo to another. Just a fraction of a second of half-light—but in that instant Wentworth had caught a glimpse of a faintly visible eye on the cabin wall directly opposite the closet—a phosphorescent eye that was half-revealed in the dimmed light!

"You are guilty as hell, Harmon!" he gritted—and his guns drew back slightly, his fingers tightened on the triggers.

"No—no, Spider! I swear to God! I couldn't help myself! I had to come here—had to do as I was told. I would have been killed otherwise. But I have done nothing; I swear to God—"

His face had frozen into a mask of abject terror. Perspiration poured out on it, ran down his cheeks, beaded his forehead and slowly brought out on his brow an almond-shaped eye, the mark of his doom!

"You must believe me, Spider," he pleaded. "I will prove what I am saying. I will tell you—"

Like a shot the Spider catapulted across the cabin and bowled him over; sent him crashing to the floor in a quivering heap. The same low-crouching dive carried Wentworth to the curtained doorway of the closet, pitched him into it headlong—to close his arms around the legs of the man who was concealed there, and tumble him and the death-ray projector he clutched out onto the cabin floor!

For a brief moment they struggled; and then the Spider was on top, an automatic jammed into the fellow's stomach. Yanking him to his feet, he tore the masking handkerchief away from the face of—Peter Ellison!

Peter Ellison, the first of the Alden-Harmon party to die when they reached New York... Peter Ellison, the friend of

Morton Cramer's, who must have known of the gem-stealing commission Cramer had received from Trueman Harmon... Peter Ellison, whose aerial and scientific inventions were many and well known....

THE SPIDER'S glittering eyes hardened as he faced his catch; eyes that revealed no surprise. "So it was you, Ellison," his discordant voice rasped jarringly. "Congratulations on an excellent job of fiendish plotting and bestial murdering! You almost got away with it, too. You would have, if you had not been so anxious to fasten the blame on that poor devil Harmon; that was your mistake. You must have made life hell for him—with that eye on his forehead to remind him of his doom whenever his skin became moist!

"What was the rest of the program? Were you going to murder Miss van Sloan—or was she to be a witness against Harmon when the Coast Guard or the Navy took this liner away from the pirates you have on board to seize it? Of course, you weren't staying on board—I know that. Probably going off on the pilot-boat, weren't you? Cutting loose and double-crossing all your dupes—and going back to share the loot with Viola Dunn, is that it?"

"Exactly, Spider," a low, deadly calm voice spoke behind him—and a gun muzzle jammed against his back. "Let me congratulate you on an excellent job of sleuthing. Don't more!" Viola Dunn snapped. "Don't move—except to raise your hands above your head!"

Silently he obeyed. Slowly his arms went up—and his automatic roared, its bullet smashing into the overhead light and plunging the cabin into darkness! Perfect coordination was the only thing that saved his life in that desperate moment. With lightning speed he flung himself to one side and whipped around to grab the girl and drag her to the floor. Her gun roared—harmlessly; and then he wrested it from her fingers, brought it down mercifully over her head.

Peter Ellison might have saved the situation in that moment—but he thought only of saving himself. Before Wentworth could grab him, the panic-stricken fiend, who had calmly ordered the murder of helpless thousands, leaped past him, through the cabin door, and bolted down the passageway.

Out onto the deck he ran, frantically seeking a place of safety—but the Spider was close at his heels. Relentlessly his ugly Nemesis closed in upon him, drove him to the rear of the upper deck. Ellison tried to run, saw that he was trapped; he sobbed in panic, but that misshapen black form came on, on....

The rear of that deck was deserted, but from below came the rattle of shots, the curses and groans of wounded and dying men, the cheers of the crew as they swept the Orientals before them. The heartless killers who had done his bidding were out of Peter Ellison's reach as the Spider's steely fingers closed on his throat

Desperately, frenziedly, Peter Ellison struggled to break loose, but now he was at the very edge of the rail, was being pressed back over the side. One frantic struggle—and he and his ebon-garbed executioner plunged overboard.

Down, down through the icy cold—and then one head broke the surface of the bay; the ugly head of a stygian figure who seemed to be part of the night as he struck out strongly into the darkness where the wavelets lapped against the side of a drifting speedboat. The Spider's mission was fulfilled, and the darkness from whence he came opened its arms to re-enfold him.

POPULAR HERO PULPS AVAILABLE NOW:

THE SPIDER
- ❏ #1: The Spider Strikes $13.95
- ❏ #2: The Wheel of Death $13.95
- ❏ #3: Wings of the Black Death $13.95
- ❏ #4: City of Flaming Shadows $13.95
- ❏ #5: Empire of Doom! $13.95
- ❏ #6: Citadel of Hell $13.95
- ❏ #7: The Serpent of Destruction $13.95
- ❏ #8: The Mad Horde $13.95
- ❏ #9: Satan's Death Blast $13.95
- ❏ #10: The Corpse Cargo $13.95
- ❏ #11: Prince of the Red Looters $13.95
- ❏ #12: Reign of the Silver Terror $13.95
- ❏ #13: Builders of the Dark Empire $13.95
- ❏ #14: Death's Crimson Juggernaut $13.95
- ❏ #15: The Red Death Rain $13.95
- ❏ #16: The City Destroyer $13.95
- ❏ #17: The Pain Emperor $13.95
- ❏ #18: The Flame Master $13.95
- ❏ #19: Slaves of the Crime Master $13.95
- ❏ #20: Reign of the Death Fiddler $13.95
- ❏ #21: Hordes of the Red Butcher $13.95
- ❏ #22: Dragon Lord of the Underworld $13.95
- ❏ #23: Master of the Death-Madness $13.95
- ❏ #24: King of the Red Killers $13.95
- ❏ #25: Overlord of the Damned $13.95
- ❏ #26: Death Reign of the Vampire King $13.95
- ❏ #27: Emperor of the Yellow Death $13.95
- ❏ #28: The Mayor of Hell $13.95
- ❏ #29: Slaves of the Murder Syndicate $13.95
- ❏ #30: Green Globes of Death $13.95
- ❏ #31: The Cholera King $13.95
- ❏ #32: Slaves of the Dragon $13.95
- ❏ #33: Legions of Madness $12.95
- ❏ #34: Laboratory of the Damned $12.95
- ❏ #35: Satan's Sightless Legion $12.95
- ❏ #36: The Coming of the Terror $12.95
- ❏ #37: The Devil's Death-Dwarfs $12.95
- ❏ #38: City of Dreadful Night $12.95
- ❏ #39: Reign of the Snake Men $12.95
- ❏ #40: Dictator of the Damned $12.95
- ❏ #41: The Mill-Town Massacres $12.95
- ❏ #42: Satan's Workshop $12.95
- ❏ #43: Scourge of the Yellow Fangs $12.95
- ❏ #44: The Devil's Pawnbroker $12.95
- ❏ #45: Voyage of the Coffin Ship $12.95

- ❏ #46: The Man Who Ruled in Hell $13.95
- ❏ #47: Slaves of the Black Monarch $13.95
- ❏ #48: Machineguns Over the White House $13.95
- ❏ #49: The City That Dared Not Eat $13.95
- ❏ #50: Master of the Flaming Horde $13.95
- ❏ #51: Satan's Switchboard $13.95
- ❏ #52: Legions of the Accursed Light $13.95
- ❏ #53: The City of Lost Men $13.95
- ❏ #54: The Grey Horde Creeps $13.95
- ❏ #55: City of Whispering Death $13.95
- ❏ #56: When Thousands Slept in Hell $13.95
- ❏ #57: Satan's Shakles $14.95
- ❏ #58: The Emperor From Hell $14.95
- ❏ #59: The Devil's Candlesticks $14.95
- ❏ #60: The City That Paid to Die $14.95
- ❏ #61: The Spider at Bay $14.95
- ❏ #62: Scourge of the Black Legions $14.95
- ❏ #63: The Withering Death $14.95
- ❏ #64: Claws of the Golden Dragon $14.95
- ❏ #65: The Song of Death $14.95
- ❏ #66: The Silver Death Reign $14.95
- ❏ ***NEW*: #67: Blight of the Blazing Eye** $14.95

THE WESTERN RAIDER
- ❏ #1: Guns of the Damned $13.95
- ❏ #2: The Hawk Rides Back from Death $13.95
- ❏ #3: Gun-Call for the Lost Legion $13.95
- ❏ #4: The Law of Silver Trent $13.95
- ❏ #5: The Gun-Prayer of Silver Trent $13.95
- ❏ #6: Silver Trent Rides Alone $13.95

G-8 AND HIS BATTLE ACES
- ❏ #1: The Bat Staffel $13.95

CAPTAIN SATAN
- ❏ #1: The Mask of the Damned $13.95
- ❏ #2: Parole for the Dead $13.95
- ❏ #3: The Dead Man Express $13.95
- ❏ #4: A Ghost Rides the Dawn $13.95
- ❏ #5: The Ambassador From Hell $13.95

DR. YEN SIN
- ❏ #1: Mystery of the Dragon's Shadow $12.95
- ❏ #2: Mystery of the Golden Skull $12.95
- ❏ #3: Mystery of the Singing Mummies $12.95